OPEN
MIC
NIGHT
AT
WESTMINSTER
CEMETERY

DEAR READER

This play, based on a true story, was originally written for the Deceased and was first performed at Westminster Cemetery in Baltimore, Maryland. All of the characters you will meet, unless explicitly identified as Living, are Dead. I would say that no animals were harmed in the making of this spectacle, but there is one tiny mouse for which I beg your forgiveness—it was an accident, as you shall see.

The debut was so well received by the grateful Dead, my intent is to "take it on the road," as they say, and perform it in cemeteries hither and yon. And to further the reach of this work even more, I have decided to recreate the play in the form you are holding now: a novel. If you are the type who insists that novels be comprised of tidy paragraphs, you will be perplexed by what lies ahead. This is no ordinary novel, you will say, this is a stage play! If you are a dramatist, you may throw your hands up and shout: For God's sake, why not write

. . . life is much too important a thing ever to talk seriously about . . .

—OSCAR WILDE

Death's an old joke, but each individual encounters it anew.

—IVAN TURGENEV

Stay there until you see you are gazing at the Light with its own ageless eyes.

—RUMI

TABLE OF CONTENTS

FOR IVAN, WHO HAS HAUNTED MANY A CEMETERY WITH ME, EVEN WHILE ON VACATION. AND FOR EVERY COURAGEOUS SOUL WHO HAS EVER STOOD—KNEES QUAKING, PALMS SWEATING, HEART POUNDING—BEFORE ANY KIND OF "OPEN MIC" TO TELL OR SING A TRUTH.

Any resemblance to actual persons, living or dead, is entirely coincidental. Yes, the Westminster Hall and Burying Ground does exist, and Edgar, Virginia, and Maria are all buried there, but if you are an historian of Poe or of the place or of the period, do not get your knickers in a twist over any inaccuracies herein. This is a work of fiction, and the author enjoyed taking many liberties along the way.

Carolrhoda Lab™
An imprint of Carolrhoda Books
A division of Lerner Publishing Group, Inc.
241 First Avenue North
Minneapolis, MN 55401 USA

For reading levels and more information, look up this title at www.lernerbooks.com.

Cover and interior images: Marcin Perkowski/Shutterstock.com (raven); Voysla/Shutterstock.com (neon letters); annamiro/Shutterstock.com (grunge letters); Curly Pat/Shutterstock.com (background patterns); Anna Poguliaeva/Shutterstock.com (Victorian ornaments); Jag_cz/Shutterstock.com (gravestones).

Main body text set in Janson Text LT Std 10.5/15.
Typeface provided by Linotype AG.

Library of Congress Cataloging-in-Publication Data

Names: Amato, Mary, author.
Title: Open mic night at Westminster Cemetery / Mary Amato.
Description: Minneapolis : Carolrhoda Lab, [2018] | Summary: Sixteen-year-old Lacy Brink, surprised to find herself dead and buried at Baltimore's Westminster Cemetery, recruits fellow poets Sam and Edgar Allan Poe in resisting tyrannical Mrs. Steele's rules by having an open mic night.
Identifiers: LCCN 2017038717 (print) | LCCN 2018007835 (ebook) | ISBN 9781541523777 (eb pdf) | ISBN 9781512465310 (th : alk. paper)
Subjects: | CYAC: Dead—Fiction. | Future life—Fiction. | Cemeteries—Fiction. | Poetry—Fiction. | Poe, Edgar Allan, 1809–1849—Fiction.
Classification: LCC PZ7.A49165 (ebook) | LCC PZ7.A49165 Op 2018 (print) | DDC [Fic]—dc23

LC record available at https://lccn.loc.gov/2017038717

Manufactured in the United States of America
1-43062-32220-4/13/2018

OPEN MIC NIGHT AT WESTMINSTER CEMETERY

A NOVEL IN TWO ACTS

MARY AMATO

olrhoda LAB
NNEAPOLIS

a normal book? Well, it is what it is. Perhaps you will be the spirited reader who enjoys it because of its oddities.

I do need to add one disclaimer: If the Living should somehow get a hold of a copy and wish to perform it, common sense should dictate how and when to alter the stage directions. A live actor playing the part of Sam should not *spoiler alert* literally stab himself in the heart, for example. The joy will be in dreaming up the stagecraft to conjure necessary special effects. In other words, do paint charming and vivid stage pictures for your audience, but do not be stupid about it. The author will not be held liable for any physical, psychological, spiritual, or intellectual damage caused by the reading or performance of this work.

ALL MY BEST. BREAK A LEG . . . OR TWO. IF YOU'RE DEAD, YOU WON'T EVEN FEEL IT.

ACT I

SCENE 1: SAM AND LACY

Lights gradually reveal a small, spooky graveyard cloaked in fog. Even though it's dark, we can make out the gothic, empty church in the center and the modern apartments and office buildings across the street. This is Westminster Cemetery in downtown Baltimore: a jumble of tilting tombstones, crumbling sarcophagi, and mold-covered crypts surrounding the old church and guarded by a black, spiked iron gate. A white, square monument stands over a family grave site near the entrance, and if we're observant, we'll notice a rather famous name on its base: Poe.

The admirers of Edgar Allan Poe who seek out this cemetery to pay their respects to the writer find the place suitably decrepit and creepy in a charming way, but we see none of them at this hour. It is midnight, and all is deathly still. The mournful toll of the bell begins.

On the third chime, a plot of earth marked with a tombstone about twenty paces toward the back of the cemetery opens like an old cellar door, and a figure climbs out. This is Sam. He is a fair-haired, gray-eyed, quietly handsome boy of seventeen uncomfortably buttoned up in his stiff, itchy Civil War uniform. As he tugs at the collar and tries to adjust the poorly fitting cap over his curls, looking hardly the soldier, we can't help doing the rough calculation: if Sam died sometime between 1861 and 1865, it would mean he has been stuck in that uniform for over 150 years, poor fellow.

From the worn leather satchel he wears around his chest he pulls out a knife and a rather antique-looking pencil. With a few deft strokes of the knife, he sharpens the pencil. Although we see the lead coming to a point, we notice that no shavings fall to the ground and we get the hint that the laws of physics must work differently among the Dead.

He puts away the knife and begins to pace, stopping every now and then to look at Edgar's grave as if for inspiration. Finally, his eyes light up. He pulls a small hand-stitched journal out of his satchel, sits on a stone bench, and begins to write a poem. As his pencil races across the page, he is ecstatic. He completes the poem and puts the last period down with a flourish. Pleased, Sam slips the pencil back into his satchel, holds his journal out in front of him, and begins reading his work silently. Unfortunately, as he reads, the look of euphoria on his face dims and then disappears. He tears the page out, crumples it, and stuffs it in a large rusty urn, long empty of flowers, smashing down all his previous discards to make room for his latest disappointment. Then he turns to Edgar's grave and moans softly.

SAM: Edgar, why can't I be like you?

With a violent sigh, he puts his journal back into his satchel, pulls out his knife, and stabs himself in the heart.

He staggers around dramatically quite a bit and then finally falls to the ground near Poe's monument with a thud.

A long pause.

We hear a caw. Raven enters, lands on the top edge of the monument, and looks down at Sam. Another pause. Raven turns and lifts his tail as if to—

SAM *(opening one eye)*: Don't you dare.

Raven turns back around and adjusts his wings. We think we see a smile at the corners of his beak, although, of course, we know that birds don't smile.

In the next moment, the south-facing side of the Poe monument swings open and words etched on that side are briefly illuminated by the moonlight for us to see: Virginia Clemm Poe, born August 15, 1822, died January 30, 1847.

The twenty-five-year-old wife of Edgar Allan Poe peeks out, and Sam quickly and respectfully removes his cap. Virginia has large dark eyes, and although most of her dark hair is neatly combed and gathered into a tight bun in the back of her head, a few loose tendrils bounce playfully around her cheeks and neck. When she sees that Sam is the only other resident up, she steps out and the door to her monument swings shut. She is forever dressed in her best, which is a modest gown in white brocade with a sash around the bodice and a full, ankle-length skirt.

Sam is always thrilled to catch a glimpse of pretty Virginia, not because he believes that he has any chance of romance with her, but because she is Edgar's wife, a woman who inspired poems from a poet's pen. Virginia knows she has his attention and milks it for all it's worth. First of all, it's amusing for her to see shy Sam squirm, and secondly, she needs Sam as an ally, as we'll soon see.

VIRGINIA *(whispering with a smile)*: Hello, Sammy. You're looking handsome tonight. Is Missus You-Know-Who up yet?

Virginia takes a step closer, and Sam blushes.

[Yes, dear Reader, the Dead do experience physical responses to stimuli; although, due to the fact that blushing in this case is caused by a rising of ethereal energy to the face rather than blood, the effect is that the cheeks appear more gray than pink.]

SAM: Not yet, Mrs. Poe.
VIRGINIA *(pouts)*: Sammy, I've been telling you for years, I hate being called "Mrs. Poe."
SAM: I'm sorry . . . Virginia.

Virginia smiles and ruffles Sam's curly hair, which he finds both electrifying and humiliating. Noticing the knife still sticking out of his chest, she gives him another patronizing smile.

VIRGINIA *(continuing to whisper)*: Aw, is Sad Sammy having trouble writing his poems again?
SAM *(quickly pulls the knife out and puts it in his satchel)*: Poems? What? I don't—
VIRGINIA: Oh Sammy. Everybody knows that you're forever scribbling in that notebook of yours and then moaning

about how your writing never turns out the way you want. Why don't you finally give up and have some fun?

SAM: But poetry is—

VIRGINIA: You want to know what I think of poetry? *(She puts her thumb on her nose and wiggles her fingers.)* Bah humbug.

SAM: But your husband—

VIRGINIA *(leaning in to whisper even softer)*: Eddy, the famous poet, was a miserable mess of a man. What did poetry ever get him, Sammy?

SAM: Fame, for one thing, Mrs.—Virginia. I thought you loved his poetry.

VIRGINIA: I did. But all he ever did was write, write, write. And what has he done ever since he died? Sleep, sleep, sleep. *(She rolls her eyes.)* As boring as yesterday's toast.

SAM *(looks over at Edgar's grave)*: Maybe he's not sleeping, Virginia. Maybe he's writing.

VIRGINIA: He could be dancing a jig down there in his unmentionables every night for all I care. I'm awake and I'm going to have a bit of recreation.

A crypt door engraved with the name Cumberland Poltroon opens and a dashing Victorian hunk peeks out dressed in a crisp waistcoat, vest, and cravat. Virginia waves. Cumberland bows to Virginia and then cautiously steps halfway out, peering around to see if anyone else is up. He nods at Sam, who doesn't care for Cumberland Poltroon but is too polite not to nod back.

VIRGINIA *(whispering to Sam)*: I know you won't tell, Sammy. Ta-ta!

Virginia blows Sam a kiss and then races over to Cumberland's crypt, giggling all the way. The two duck inside, and the door closes with a faint creak. Sam sighs heavily, shoves on his cap, and throws himself on the ground, certain that he can't write a poem worth reciting; certain that he will never have a friend, let alone a girlfriend; certain that tonight will be just another boring stretch like every other one that has come before it for the last 150 years.

There is a long moment of silence, and then an abrupt change comes over Raven. The bird's neck stretches and he blinks as if being called to action. His claws grip the edge of the monument on which he's perched and his body rises up to its full height. He spreads his wings and squawks majestically.

RAVEN: Lacy Brink. Lacy Brink.
SAM *(sits up, shocked)*: What?
RAVEN *(squawking)*: Lacy Brink. Lacy Brink.

Flustered, Sam gets up and stares incredulously at the bird.

SAM: What exactly do you mean by "Lacy Brink"? It can't be a name.

Raven shrugs and folds his wings. Sam looks around, wanting to wake up someone to talk about it with, but the sad truth is that there is no one in the cemetery Sam would call a friend. Finally, he begins to search the grounds for the unthinkable: a new grave. Puzzled, he talks to Raven as he looks.

SAM: This is ridiculous. There can't be a new grave. We're officially closed. We haven't had a new resident since 1913. It can't—

Raven notices what Sam does not . . . a shifting of the earth near a stone bench just a few yards from Poe's monument. Raven clears his throat and Sam turns. A rough circle of earth is pushed up and over, revealing a hole, much the way the carved lid of a jack-o'-lantern can be lifted to reveal the scooped-out interior of the pumpkin. To Sam's amazement, a moment later, sixteen-year-old Lacy Brink climbs out of the hole. Dazed, she stands and instinctively brushes off her very short skirt, bare legs, boots, and short wool jacket.

Sam catches glimpses of the Living from time to time—they tend to be faces passing by in cars or uninteresting men who stumble in the street past the cemetery in the middle of the night or even drunk ones who wander into the cemetery in need of a snore—but he has not seen a recently Deceased person up close since the last burial at Westminster, which was old James Hirston in 1913. And in all the years before that, none of the souls who rose from their graves ever looked like this girl. Her frizzy dark hair is wild. Her expression is serious. She's guarded, but vulnerable at the same time.

The girl looks around, trying to determine if she could still be in a dream. She knows this cemetery well—it's Westminster, which has been a daytime hangout of hers for years—but it's late and she has no memory of walking here. She wonders if she might have sleepwalked. The strangely dressed boy staring at her isn't helping. Possible explanations flit through her mind: he could be one of those Civil War reenactor geeks on his way home from a rehearsal, or maybe an actor on his way home from a performance. The Hippodrome Theater is right around the corner, after all. She considers the thought that it might be Halloween night. It is October, isn't it? For some reason, she can't even remember. She checks her pockets for her cell phone and discovers it isn't there. Unnerved, she begins a panicky search for the phone on the ground around the stone bench.

SAM *(respectfully removing his cap)*: Um . . . miss . . . are you . . .

Sam can't possibly compose a coherent sentence. To see so much of a girl his own age is overwhelming. He wants to drink in every inch of her, but he is too shy to take in anything but furtive peeks. Her face is so dynamic. Her legs and neck are so bare. Her jacket is open and the soft black shirt she is wearing with her short skirt is stretched tight across her chest. He quickly looks down at the cap in his hand and stammers.

SAM: You must be . . . Raven announced a name, which is what happens when a new resident wakes up . . . I . . . I can't believe it . . . I didn't think that we could get any more new residents.

LACY *(completely confused)*: New resident?

SAM: Well, of course, there must be some mistake, miss. I . . . I know you can't be a new resident. We've been closed to new residents for years, and you're so . . . new.

Sam finally allows himself to look up. They lock eyes, and a joyous warmth rushes through him.

Struck by his soulful gaze, Lacy feels the spark of attraction, but then she tells herself she's being ridiculous. She's alone and it's dark. She should be alert. She glances through the iron gate at the street beyond the cemetery and tries to guess how late it is. She remembers that she was on her way to Tenuto's Coffee House for the open mic and wonders if she stopped in here and blacked out for a moment. She left home around seven or eight, didn't she? The stillness of the street is interrupted only by the occasional passing car. It looks more like midnight or later. The foyer light of the apartment building across the street is on. Just a block down, the hospital is open, of course. If she screams, someone will come and help, she says to herself, and decides it's worth the risk to stay and try to find her cell phone. If this guy is nice, maybe he'll even help. She tries to keep her voice light and confident.

LACY: I'm just looking for my cell phone, which must be around here . . .

SAM: Cell phone? May I ask what that is?

Lacy gives him an odd glance, not knowing if he is trying to stay in character for a Civil War soldier or if he is certifiably crazy, and quickly intensifies her search.

Sam and Raven exchange glances. The thought of someone like her, a Modern girl his own age, joining the community fills Sam with joy. Although it has been a long time since a new resident emerged from his or her grave at Westminster, Sam recalls how confused and disoriented some were at first. Perhaps if he can find what she is looking for, she will see him as her first friend here at Westminster. Eager but shy, he stands hesitantly, unsure of how to proceed. Raven nods his head at Sam, encouraging him to try.

SAM *(to Lacy)*: If . . . if you tell me what it looks like, perhaps I can help you, miss.

Lacy gives him another incredulous look, wondering why he's trying to keep up the act. She ignores him and continues looking for her phone. When she realizes it's not there, she explodes.

LACY: Fuck.

Sam's eyes grow wide, and Raven winces. They know what's coming. Sure enough, through the fog from the back of the cemetery near the spot where Sam first appeared, a plot of earth opens and a woman marches out. She is a straight-backed, older woman wearing a long, plain black dress, tight at the throat and tight at the cuffs. Her long gray hair is braided and wound into a bun that looks as if it has been nailed in place on the top of her head. Her self-righteous zeal gives her remarkable energy and speed and so it only seems to take her a second before she appears at Sam's side. This is Gertrude Steele.

MRS. STEELE: I heard a most obscene word.

Mrs. Steele stares disapprovingly at Lacy's bare skin, her skimpy clothes, and her wild, unorthodox hair.

Lacy steps back, her mind racing to piece together an explanation for what seems to be another very authentically costumed character.

MRS. STEELE *(turns to Sam)*: Who in heaven's name is this?
SAM *(straightening up nervously)*: This is a new resident, ma'am. I believe she's a Modern.
MRS. STEELE *(her face twisting into a sour shape)*: A Modern? How did she get in?
SAM: She's a new resident. Raven announced her. *(He nods toward the bird, who is still perched on Poe's monument.)*
MRS. STEELE: Impossible. Raven made a mistake.

Offended, Raven squawks. The bird and the old woman glower at each other for a moment.

MRS. STEELE *(turning back to Sam)*: She must have escaped from some other cemetery, God knows how, and snuck in here. *(Fixing a cold stare at Lacy)* Go back to your own place. We don't want your kind. If you were a resident here at Westminster, I would give you a strike for that terrible language and a strike for your *(looks her up and down again)* completely vulgar outfit.
SAM: Strikes can't be given for clothing, ma'am. Remember, we have no choice in that.
MRS. STEELE: Well, she looks like a prostitute.
LACY *(stares at Mrs. Steele in shock)*: I can't believe you just said that to my face. I don't even know you.

Sam wants desperately to defend her, to tell her that she looks fascinating, but he doesn't dare say anything that will anger Mrs. Steele. Lacy gives them both what she thinks will be one last look, turns, and walks to the iron gate.

SAM: It won't work. We can open our crypt and coffin doors and manipulate things we were buried with, but we cannot manipulate anything else—

Lacy grabs hold of the gate handle. It's strange. She is touching it and yet she can't exactly feel it. She pulls. It won't open. She pushes. It won't budge.

LACY: Fuck.

Sam winces.

MRS. STEELE *(steps forward to shake a menacing finger at Lacy)*: That would be strike two! You are lucky you are not a resident here, young lady. *(Turning to Sam)* How on earth did she get in, anyway? Samuel, is there a problem with the gate?

LACY *(her voice rising)*: Yes, there is a problem with the gate! I can't get out. *(She turns back around and begins to push and pull violently.)* What the fu—

SAM *(jumping forward to stop her from swearing again)*: Fulcrum! *(He turns to Mrs. Steele.)* She doesn't understand the rules, ma'am, but she is a new resident. I saw it myself. She emerged right here. *(He runs over and points to the unmarked spot by the stone bench.)* Her grave is small and there's no proper door. My guess is that she was cremated and that someone buried her ashes here.

At the mention of words such as "grave" and "ashes," Lacy is completely spooked. Since she can't seem to get out the front, she runs to the back of the cemetery and, finding no exit, runs all the way around it. Unlike most churches, which have neat adjoining cemeteries to one side or behind, the graves at Westminster are sprinkled around all four sides of the property. Most of the Dead, including Poe and his family, are buried in the prestigious main section to the right of the church, the one where Lacy first found herself and the one where Sam and Mrs. Steele are now. But what Lacy finds as she runs is an obstacle course of crypts, tombstones, and statuary bordered on all sides by either the iron gate or brick walls.

As Lacy's panic grows, Mrs. Steele continues to talk to Sam.

MRS. STEELE: Clearly her people put her here with no regard for the rules, Samuel. We don't have to accept her. Don't read the Official Welcome. Just look at her. She's vulgar.

Sam does what everyone in Westminster does: he plays it safe and pretends to agree with Mrs. Steele, but he does so in a whisper, hoping that Lacy won't hear him.

SAM: She is a bit vulgar, ma'am, but I think we have to welcome her. I think there's a rule—

MRS. STEELE *(interrupting)*: Thinking and knowing are as different as bats and bluebirds, Samuel. What number is the rule, *hmmn?* You should have them all memorized. You've had decade after decade to study, but instead all you've been doing is wallowing—writing silly nonsense in that journal of yours.

Sam bites his lip. Flustered, he pulls a small scroll from his pocket, accidentally drops the bottom bar, and a long sheet of parchment unrolls until it hits the unkempt grass with a thud. An arm emerges from the grave on which Sam is standing and hands the bottom of the scroll back up to him. Lacy, still trying to get out, is spared the sight. She has jumped down from a crypt and is trying now to climb the tall iron gate directly. With her back to them, her beautiful bare legs are even more visible.

Both Mrs. Steele and Sam watch her, knowing she won't be able to leave. The expression on Mrs. Steele's face could scare a rottweiler. Sam, on the other hand, is clearly and completely smitten. Mrs. Steele notices his enthusiasm and gives him a hard slap across the head.

MRS. STEELE: See? Girls like that cause problems. They absolutely inspire thoughts of lust. It's a disgrace. Get a hold of yourself, Samuel. We're not going to welcome her.

SAM *(quickly turning his attention to the scroll)*: I'm just recalling a rule, ma'am.

Sam scans the scroll and finds what he's looking for. Inwardly delighted, he makes sure not to show it. Pretending to be upset, he turns toward her.

SAM: Unfortunately, it's right here, ma'am. Rule 17: The Living are held accountable for decisions involving burial as well as the dispersal of ashes. Although the Dying may leave explicit instructions, the Dead are powerless to execute those instructions. Thus, in the case of a procedural error or an illegal burial, the Deceased Community must receive the newly interred resident with an Official Welcome and cannot exclude anyone because of race, religion, or lack of fame or fortune. *(Looks up)* I have no choice, ma'am. I have to give her the Official Welcome. It's my job.

Mrs. Steele's eyes narrow and she lets out a huff.

MRS. STEELE: Well. If we have to welcome her, then at least it will be a very short residence. She already has two strikes.

SAM: Strikes can only be given after the first ten rules have been read. That is Rule 11. It's coming back to me, ma'am. I do know some of them by heart.

MRS. STEELE *(irritated)*: You are right. Do your duties then.

Sam glances at the distraught Lacy, who is back at the main gate trying to get out again.

SAM: Now? But . . . she doesn't seem to be listening . . .

MRS. STEELE *(with a cold smile)*: Exactly. The quicker she is welcomed, the quicker she'll get her strikes.

SAM: What about the Welcome Song? It's supposed to come before I recite the rules. The song was Mrs. Watson's duty, but she's been Suppressed.

MRS. STEELE: Do it! Rule 221 states that in case of emergency, one resident may perform a duty for another. The sooner we act, the quicker this problem will be solved. *(She gestures to his scroll.)* Do the song and the first ten rules, but do not fraternize or . . . *(whispers)* help her in any way.

I'm going to wake our President of the Committee on the Preservation of the Documentation of Rules and Regulations and we'll go to the vault to read over the original documents. There must be a rule in my favor. If someone's presence degrades our collective respectability, we should be able to permanently isolate that someone and remove any and all aboveground privileges. In the meantime . . . *(again, she drops her voice to a whisper)* encourage her to rant and rave. That foul mouth of hers will get her three strikes in no time.

With a swish of her black skirts, Mrs. Steele turns and walks through the fog toward the church's back brick wall. The catacomb entrance is there, a portal invisible to the Living that leads to the subterranean maze of burial vaults under the church, where the first residents were laid to rest and where the documents related to the genesis of the cemetery have been kept since the earliest of days. As Mrs. Steele approaches, a door-shaped section of the church wall seems to swing open, and she disappears inside.

Sam would like to take his time, find a way to gently win Lacy's trust before barraging her with the rules, but he doesn't dare disobey Mrs. Steele.

He unrolls the scroll and approaches the girl.

SAM: Um . . . I'm not the one who usually sings the Welcome Song, but . . . it is supposed to come before the Reading of the Rules, and so here it is . . .

With a shaky voice, Sam sings.

Every flow'r doth bloom and fade with time.
Every beast shall cease its uphill climb.
So with grace must thou accept thy lot—
Thy soul escapes the body's worm and rot.
May thou slumber in thy earthly bed—
Ne'er to toil in need of daily bread.
Naught to grasp or covet, naught to fear.
Now the steady virtue and good cheer.
Protest not, the aim of death is true.
So to Westminster, we welcome you.

Lacy turns around and stares. The mean-spirited woman has disappeared and now this odd guy is singing to her. This whole episode keeps getting stranger and stranger, she thinks. Exhausted from her fruitless attempt to climb the gate, she leans back against it. The guy hasn't touched her. Hasn't tried to stop her from leaving. If he wanted to grab her or murder her, he could have done that by now. Hell, she thinks, she could probably kick his ass.

[Offensive words, I know! Please note, dear Reader, that when I'm relaying the internal thoughts of a character, I must use his or her choice of words, undignified as they might be.]

Lacy looks off to the southeast corner of the street. The fog has lifted slightly and the lights of the nearby hospital are visible now. It occurs to her that the guy and woman could be patients who escaped from the psych ward to come here and fulfill some weird but probably harmless ghost delusion. If she plays along, perhaps the guy can show her how to get the gate open, she thinks.

Relieved that she is calming down, Sam continues in his official capacity.

SAM *(unrolling more of the scroll)*: And now, the Recitation of the Ten Rules of Etiquette. They are very important, miss. *(He leans toward Lacy, his face full of concern, and reads.)*

Rule 1: Residents will refrain from uttering profanities and/or obscenities.

Rule 2: With the exception of the Town Crier, there will be no raising of the voice. No screaming, no yelling, no wailing.

Rule 3: Boundaries must be observed. No resident is allowed to either temporarily or permanently enter another resident's burial space, whether that be coffin, crypt, sarcophagus, urn, et cetera.

Rule 4: Residents with aboveground privileges may rise at midnight to enjoy appropriate recreation but must return to the earth before the sun rises and remain there until midnight.

Lacy listens, trying to puzzle out exactly what the story is. The boy seems dead serious. Perhaps he's not insane, she thinks. Perhaps he's doing some kind of candid camera show. Reflexively, she looks around, expecting to see a video crew lurking behind a tree. She had heard of some Icelandic artist who once did an installation in a cemetery involving actors.

She notices that the large black bird perched on the monument seems to be watching her. Could it be a stuffed decoy hiding a surveillance camera? she wonders.

Raven gives her a disarming wink.

SAM *(continues reading)*:

Rule 5: All residents will be assigned a job and must do their job without complaint.

Rule 6: Neatness in appearance shows a discipline of character. Although residents cannot choose their burial attire, care must be taken not to allow one's clothing to become slovenly or unnecessarily revealing.

Rule 7: Do not argue about politics or religion.

Rule 8: Gentlemen should either bow or tip their hats or remove their hats entirely upon greeting a lady. Upon meeting a lady for the first time or being reunited with one after a long separation, a gentleman may take a lady's hand in his for a few seconds. The show of a kiss to the hand can be made, but lips should touch only gloved hands.

Rule 9: If you have remarkably fine teeth, you may smile freely; if not, you should avoid smiling.

Rule 10: A lady should only take the arm of a gentleman to which she is not related in cases in which it is necessary—as in passing through a crowd, over uneven terrain, or if likely to faint.

Sam notices that the girl is giving him a strange look, as if she doesn't quite believe him, but he keeps going.

SAM: A resident who breaks any of the above rules will be given a strike, and residents who receive three strikes become Suppressed. *(He tries to catch her attention. This is important.)* That means you lose aboveground privileges. That means you can't come out, miss. Ever. Again.

At this last bit, Lacy is weirdly touched. This guy seems to be genuinely worried about her. Out of the corner of her eye, through the fog, she can see a car pull up at the apartment building on the other side of the street and a couple walk from the car to the building's front door. They are dressed in what to Lacy are ordinary clothes, a couple coming home from a night on the town. The sight reminds her that she's not isolated. It calms her down. She'll keep an eye out. If she needs to, she can call for help.

SAM *(concluding)*: There are 247 other rules related to how things work around here, and it's the responsibility of the resident to read and study the other 247 rules on his or her own, but these first ten are the ones you must memorize. *(Sam steps forward and holds out the scroll to Lacy.)*

Lacy decides to humor him. She smiles uneasily and takes it.

LACY: Thank you so much . . . Samuel, is it? . . . I can tell you're trying to help. That was a very nice song and everything. And I can see that the rules of your game—or whatever it is—are really important to you. But I need to get back home. Please just tell me how to unlock the gate. *(She forces herself to fake a laugh.)* I'm really bad with locks. I can never get my locker open.

SAM: None . . . none of us can leave. It's just . . . it's just how it works, Miss Brink.

The sound of her last name coming out of Sam's mouth sends a chill through Lacy. She has never seen this guy before in her life. She knows that for certain.

LACY: You know my name?

SAM: Lacy Brink.

Lacy drops the scroll. Before Sam can stop her, she opens her mouth and lets out a scream loud enough to wake the Dead. Sam jumps in a panic. Through the catacomb portal, Mrs. Steele marches out. She can tell by Sam's face that he has already read the first ten rules.

MRS. STEELE *(triumphantly raising a bony finger)*: Rule 2: No screaming or raising of the voice. Strike one!

SCENE 2: REALITY SINKS IN

As I said, Lacy's scream is loud enough to wake the Dead, and that is precisely what is happening. Shocked faces emerge from eleven graves, four crypts, and three sarcophagi, most frightened, some concerned, some dull with the assumption that one of the old residents has finally lost it and there's nothing to be done, and some so starved for novelty that they look excited.

The pretty face of Virginia Poe falls into that latter category. Since she is breaking a rule by being in the Poltroon crypt, she can only afford to peek. We don't see her partner in crime, Cumberland Poltroon, who is cowering behind, the fact of which is making her remember why she has no respect for him.

While it was disturbing enough for Lacy to see so many faces pop out, three of the faces belong to Suppressed souls and thus an even more disturbing action occurs. Against the church's side wall, Lacy sees what she thinks are the crumbled ruins of a statue rise up and take the shape of a strong, broad-shouldered, thick-limbed boy. As he walks forward, she realizes that there was no transformation of stone. He is a person, just like the rest of them, only he had been sitting motionless on the remains of a broken tombstone near the wall for so long, her mind had tricked her. This is Owen Hapliss, the cemetery's Suppressor, an eighteen-year-old blacksmith who had spent the majority of his young life pounding iron into submission. Without a single glance at any of those standing, he walks heavily toward a grave. The first Suppressed face sees him and sinks below ground just as Owen's boot slams down upon his door. Without a pause, he walks to another grave and does the same. The third face has already disappeared below, and so Owen returns to his position and Lacy shivers to see him again seem to turn to stone.

Raven, a silent witness, watches from his perch next to Sam on Poe's monument.

Mrs. Steele reels around, her mind spinning, near to panic. The fact that not one but three of the Suppressed tried to emerge confirms her instincts about this girl: her very presence here is causing turmoil. From time to time, one of the Suppressed tries to rise, of course, which is why the Suppressor is necessary; but Mrs. Steele can't remember a time when three emerged at once. Willing her face to hide any sign of weakness or concern, she turns toward the others.

MRS. STEELE: Everything is under control. There is nothing to see here. Go back to sleep! *(At this, the remaining faces withdraw and doors to the graves and crypts close. She notices that the scroll is on the ground and scowls at Sam to pick it up.)* All we need are two more strikes. Do not speak with the girl, Samuel. Ignoring her is the best option at present. Just continue with the routine. Leave her be and go back to sleep. I will take care of it. I'm returning to the catacombs.

I haven't found anything yet, but Mr. Chesterton and I are only halfway through.

The ancient-looking face of Hiram Chesterton, with just a wisp of white hair on his thin bald head, peers out of the catacomb entrance. He peels his stunned eyes off Lacy, nods at Sam, and retreats into the shadows.

With another swish of her skirts, Mrs. Steele is gone. Once again, it's just Sam and Lacy. Sam stands by the stone bench, kneading his cap in his hands. Lacy has instinctively backed up against the gate. He can see the fear in her eyes and it's breaking his heart. He wants to assure her that everything will be all right, but there is little hope of that and he does not dare address her directly. Not knowing what else to do, he begins walking to his grave.

The possibility of Sam's departure rouses Lacy from her state of shock.

LACY: Wait! How do you know my name? Why are you telling me my ashes are here? Is this some kind of sick joke?

SAM *(whispers)*: Please keep your voice down . . . for your own good.

The light in Sam's eyes and the earnest ache in his voice touch Lacy. In his poorly fitting uniform, he looks like a lost soul, not a murderer. He does want to help her, she can see it in his eyes.

For Sam's part, the gaze from Lacy is like a drink of ambrosia. It fills him and makes him want to pull out his journal and write a poem about the glint of moonlight on her face. He hasn't felt this way since . . . Abigail.

[A bit of backstory, dear Reader. From the time Sam was six until long after the day he died, he had a crush on a quiet girl named Abigail who lived down the street from their house. One of the saddest aspects of the afterlife for him has been to feel that longing for Abigail fade. But now, as you can tell, a new interest and desire is springing up inside his soul.]

Lacy decides that the best thing she can do is calm down and think. She begins to pace, realizing that any theory involving mental patients is too far-fetched considering she just saw more people in historical dress hiding out among the tombstones. She thinks she can see some of them now, peering out again.

An explanation for him knowing her name pops into her brain. Perhaps the guy—Sam—found her phone on the ground. If so, all he had to do was swipe once and the name Lacy Brink would pop up. Her mom was always telling her to put a lock on her phone, which she still hadn't done. Another idea comes to her regarding his outfit and demeanor. The perfect explanation. She quickly turns to Sam.

LACY: I get it! This is a role-playing game. The rules, the props, the costumes. I bet this is a new hyped-up zombie thing.

She is almost giddy as she realizes that this would explain everything, including why Sam and the others haven't felt like a real threat. They aren't. They're just super serious gamers. She looks around. Yes, a few more of them are peering out, listening. She tries a smile and a compliment.

LACY: Your costumes look awesome, by the way. You guys all look totally authentic. And the fog! Did you rent a fog machine or did you just get lucky?

Sam looks at the catacomb entrance. He wants to answer her but is afraid that he'll get caught. Perched on a tombstone behind the girl, Raven catches Sam's eye and mimes writing with one wing. Sam's eyes light up.

SAM: She said to "continue with the routine"! My routine isn't to go back to sleep. My routine is to write!

Quickly Sam pulls out his journal, writes a message, and hands it to Lacy.

LACY *(reading)*: "I don't want to be rude. But for the time being, it is safer not to speak directly to you." *(She hands it back.)* Wow. You're taking this game seriously, Sam.

Sam writes more and hands it back.

LACY *(reading)*: "It is not a game. It is serious, Miss Brink. Now that you've been welcomed, you can get more strikes. By the way, they aren't costumes, miss. These are the clothes we were buried in. It's common for new residents to be confused—especially ones who didn't see death coming." *(She hands him the journal again.)* I got to say, Sam, your ability to stay in character is amazing, and that's obviously one of the rules. And your costumes and props are totally legit, but I think you guys are the ones who are confused about me. You obviously think I'm one of you—a new player or actor or zombie or "resident" or whatever you call yourselves—and maybe people you don't know show up to play, but I didn't come here to play. I'm here by accident.

Convinced she is correctly piecing it all together, Lacy starts to pace, searching her memory.

LACY: I was at home getting dressed. I remember that. I was excited because there was another open mic at Tenuto's and I was trying to get up the courage to perform. I had gone twice in the summer to hear the other poets and it was amazing. The show was going to start at nine o'clock. I must have walked. Or maybe Olivia drove me? No, I must have walked. I must have decided to stop in here on my way to write a new poem and—

At the mention of the word *poem*, Sam is ecstatic. He knew she was a kindred spirit. He looks at Raven and mouths: "She writes poetry!" Lacy is too caught up to notice. She looks around the familiar old cemetery, as if seeing it for the first time. Then she continues talking, more to herself than to Sam.

LACY: Of course I would stop here! It's Westminster! But it was probably dark, and I'm only used to the cemetery in the day. I must have come in here and I must have tripped on something. *(She looks around at the crumbling brick pathway and the jumble of protruding headstones.)* Of course! I tripped and hit my head. I must have blacked out.

She turns to Sam, sure that this explanation will be understood by him, too. By all of them. She can tell some of them are still spying. They'll have to realize that she isn't a part of the game they're playing.

LACY: This has been my hangout ever since seventh grade. *(She walks over to Poe's monument and pats it affectionately, beginning to relax and loosen up now that a plausible explanation is taking shape.)* After my teacher brought us here on a field trip, I got all excited because I realized that it was closer to our house than I thought. I started stopping in here at least once a week after school to sit by myself and write poems. I thought it was cool and goth. I was kind of goth, but not really. I was too sweet to be really goth. *(She walks around the monument.)* Anyway, I've been coming ever since. It's a nice place, in a creepy way. I mean, it's quiet and it definitely has a poetic vibe, and Liv—that's my sister—and her friends are always at our house. It's easier to write here than there. I can see why you guys have chosen this place. It's great.

Sam has been listening in wonder. He doesn't know the meaning of "open mic" or "goth," but to think that this amazing girl haunted his very own cemetery during the day . . . writing poems, no less . . . is wonderful! Sam wants to tear open the locked door of his heart and confess his own desire to write poetry, but he does not have the nerve.

A few other residents have dared to peer out again. It is impossible to know how many are listening. From a crypt marked Hosler, a door creaks all the way open and a distinguished gentleman steps out wearing a black suit, black tie, white shirt, and top hat. Meet Dr. Hosler. Since his medical students affectionately buried his black leather medical bag with him, he carries it now, still at the ready. Dr. Hosler nods at Sam. They whisper.

SAM: Dr. Hosler!

DR. HOSLER: What do we have here, Samuel?

SAM: A new resident. Miss Brink. A Modern.

DR. HOSLER *(tipping his hat to Lacy)*: Miss Brink. Quite extraordinary. Medical cause of expiration?

SAM: She can't seem to remember that. She doesn't quite understand yet that she's dead. I tried to explain.

LACY: Very funny. Ha ha. You don't have to keep the charade going. I get it.

DR. HOSLER *(to Sam)*: It's been a while since we've had a new resident, but I do recall that proof helped to speed the psychological adjustment process for quite a few. I thought I'd hop out and give her the treatment and then hop back in. Mrs. Steele needn't be the wiser. Could help.

SAM: Thank you, Doctor.

Before Lacy can respond, the old doctor pulls a long surgical knife out of his bag and plunges it into her heart.

DR. HOSLER: There!

They both turn and look at Lacy. She is standing, shocked, the knife sticking out of her chest, realizing that she feels no pain. There is a long pause.

Raven whistles a funeral march.

DR. HOSLER: See, Sam, reality is sinking in. Remember, it always takes a few moments.

Sam and Dr. Hosler sit on the bench and watch with interest. Knife protruding from her chest, Lacy walks to Poe's monument and puts one hand on it to steady herself. With the other hand, she removes the knife, feeling nothing. She examines her chest for blood but there is none. She checks to see if the blade is designed to collapse or play a trick. It is not. It is as sturdy and sharp as can be.

DR. HOSLER *(stands and holds out his arms)*: Go ahead. Stab me.

SAM: Remember, we're not supposed to fraternize with her, sir.

DR. HOSLER: I'm not fraternizing. I'm proving a point. This is science.

Lacy hesitates and Dr. Hosler takes her hand with the knife and plunges it into his own chest.

DR. HOSLER: See?

Lacy steps back.

DR. HOSLER *(pulling out the knife and returning it to his bag)*: There you have it, Miss Brink. You're one of us. We can't be killed because we're already as dead as a bucket of nails. Now, quite naturally, you'll begin to psychologically adjust to your new situation. It's remarkable, really, how adaptable we are.

Satisfied, Dr. Hosler sits back down next to Sam. Lacy looks at Sam. Just as the doctor predicted, reality is sinking in. She walks around slowly, extending her arms to look at them. She still feels the flexing of her muscles. She still feels the pounding of her heart, the rush of blood to her face, the lump in her throat when she swallows, the tears threatening to gather and rise. But she is different. It's a sensation she has been aware of and subconsciously trying to deny ever since she found herself in the cemetery, a sensation that something fundamental about her body has changed, a sensation like nothing she has ever experienced: an absence, on the cellular level, of need. Now she takes off her coat and drops it on the ground. Standing only in her T-shirt, short skirt, and boots, she touches the skin of her arms and then her thighs. It feels like skin to her and yet her body is not reacting to the October cold. She takes a deep breath and blows. She feels the air expel, but no puff is visible. She puts her hand over her heart and closes her eyes. It feels like it's racing, but there's not a single thump. She stops and turns to face Sam.

LACY: I feel different, but I still feel alive.
SAM: Soldiers who have lost a limb in battle often continue to feel that limb after it's gone. It's a bit like that.
DR. HOSLER: We aren't physiologically alive, but our psyches create a simulacrum of that state.

She pinches herself hard. And then harder.

LACY: I'm dead?
SAM: Yes.

She is quiet for a moment, and then a huge blast of rage releases in a scream.

LACY: Fuck!

Sam jumps up in a panic, and Dr. Hosler hurries back to his crypt. Just as his door shuts, Mrs. Steele marches out from the catacombs.

MRS. STEELE *(thrilled)*: Strike two!

Lacy's mind is reeling.

LACY: Go to he—
SAM *(jumps forward)*: Helsinki!

SCENE 3: THE TEA

Fogs come and go, most often gradually. The fog that has been infiltrating the nooks and crannies of Westminster Cemetery lifts suddenly and wafts away, as if called to eavesdrop on some other souls, and a sharp, dark chill seems to be left in its wake.

Surrounded by graves, standing tall in her stiff black dress with her hands clasped together just under her bosom and her stern face cemented above it, Mrs. Steele looks to Lacy like one of those old-fashioned paintings in haunted houses whose eyes follow you wherever you go.

Never in her young life did Lacy feel the kind of revulsion for someone that she is feeling for this judgmental, intolerant brick of a woman standing in front of her, and she knows the woman can tell.

Mrs. Steele takes two steps toward Lacy and lifts her chin.

MRS. STEELE: Go ahead, Miss Brink. Say whatever you want to me.

Mrs. Steele's eyes flare with confidence. She'll break the girl. She has made grown men sob.

Behind Mrs. Steele, Sam waves silently to Lacy and begins a desperate charade of buttoning his lips tight as a warning. It's such a kind act on Sam's part, and one that he believes is clearly necessary.

But here's the thing: that sustained penetrating glare from Mrs. Steele is having a paradoxical effect on Lacy; it's igniting the girl's inner core, a red-hot ember of strength. It's the part of Lacy that—in life—responded to adversity by leaping into flame, giving her the fuel to move and act and survive. It ignited when she was three weeks old, fighting a virulent bacterial infection; it burned at five years of age when a strange man discovered she had become separated from her family at an amusement park and tried to take her by the hand to his car; it raged when fourth-grade bullies ambushed her after school to steal her new shoes. It grew even stronger in middle school, when cruelty oozed through the hallways every day like toxic sludge and when being allowed to ride city buses by herself meant that she would come up against challenging moments: the rants of mentally ill homeless people, the creepy guys who would unzip their pants, and once even the stabbing of a man by a woman impaired by opiate consumption. When the fire inside Lacy burned, it said: You are strong, girl. Something is happening right now that is not good; the sooner that you accept what is happening, the sooner you can figure out how to survive it.

Now, as Lacy feels this familiar inner core wake up, her soul expands so that there's space to take in this strange new reality. This is no game, no hoax, no dream. She is dead among the Dead and the rules of behavior in this afterworld can't be ignored. As bad luck would have it, she has an enemy. But she also has an ally in Sam, who is right now, in his own adorable way, reminding her to watch her mouth; and having a friend, even a frightened one, is energizing. Lacy Brink is not going to let this woman take her down. She takes a step forward and returns Mrs. Steele's gaze.

A flicker of shock at Lacy's fearlessness passes through Mrs. Steele, visible only in a brief fluttering of her eyelids. Determined not to acknowledge it, the old woman raises her chin, squares her shoulders, and wills herself not to blink.

The seconds tick by.

A breathless grin of admiration for Lacy is spreading on Sam's face, and Raven gives a similarly approving nod.

After a few more tense seconds, it's Mrs. Steele who breaks off the stare-down. With a huff, she turns to address Sam, who immediately wipes the grin off.

MRS. STEELE: I'm not worried. Not in the slightest. However, to ensure safety and tranquility in the community, I believe the less contact with the girl the better, which means that tea service should be suspended.

At this, gasps and rustlings underground are heard. It sounds to Lacy as if people are turning in their graves. Lacy looks to Sam for an explanation, but he doesn't dare say a word.

The Hosler crypt door opens and again the good doctor emerges. He tips his top hat to the women.

DR. HOSLER: Good evening, Mrs. Steele, and pardon the interruption, but I couldn't help overhearing. As President of the Committee for Safety and Tranquility, I feel as if it is my duty to respectfully suggest moving forward with our customary tea. As you said earlier—I apologize, but again I couldn't help overhearing—we should retain our usual routine. *(He steps in and whispers.)* It is only a handful of residents who rise for tea, but for those residents it is the one and only thing they look forward to. Suspending the service may result in a bit of . . . well . . . unrest. I believe you've also said, "There's nothing that a cup of tea can't put to right." Your words of wisdom, Mrs. Steele.

Dr. Hosler's speech acts as a kind of tranquilizer to Mrs. Steele. Her face doesn't exactly soften, but she isn't biting back.

Lacy, feeling victorious over the stare-down, is gathering more strength, telling herself to pay attention, to take this strike thing seriously, to make every observation count, to figure out quickly who here is friend and who is foe.

Before another word is spoken, the door on the north-facing side of Poe's monument, the one marked Maria Clemm, opens and a tall woman steps out of the shadows. It is a curious moment for Lacy because she recognizes the woman from old photographs she saw online when she did research as a seventh-grader for a report on Poe. Why she should be able to remember that and not a single detail about how her own death is one of memory's many mysteries.

At any rate, you should know that the woman marching over to join the little club is none other than Maria Clemm, Poe's mother-in-law and the mother of the young Virginia. At eighty-one, she is wearing the same thing she wore in all the photographs that Lacy saw online, the same thing she wore for too many years while she was alive: an often-mended black dress and starched white bonnet. She's all-business, the type of woman who would not wait around for a man to pull her mule out of the mud. But Lacy catches something friendly in her eye—a dormant impish spark.

MARIA: Good evening, everyone. Like Dr. Hosler, I couldn't help overhearing. Mrs. Steele, I hope you'll agree to tea. We do look forward to it.

MRS. STEELE: Good evening, Mrs. Clemm. I can see the point. Samuel, fetch Sarah.

Lacy watches Sam walk over to a plot of four modest headstones, two tall and two tiny. He knocks on the tall headstone marked Sarah Brown and a neat door of earth opens. A young woman hesitantly emerges. This is nineteen-year-old Sarah, a bashful young woman with the kindest of hearts who died in 1782. She wears the plain brown dress of a fish seller's wife with her only nice thing—a white lace shawl—tied around her shoulders. Her hair is tucked into a plain white cap.

SAM: Mrs. Brown, this is Miss Lacy Brink. She is a new resident.

MRS. STEELE: Stop it, Samuel. Introductions are not necessary. I'm quite sure everyone has heard exactly what is going on by now. Sarah, tea as usual. And then to your graves. Unfortunately Mr. Chesterton and I didn't find anything in the statutes that will be helpful in immediately resolving this problem. Samuel is correct in that, according to our rules, we must accept her into Westminster. Since she has already received the Official Welcome, the next task to come is assigning her a committee position. Mrs. Clemm, I'd like to confer with you in the catacombs.

Maria struggles to hide her disappointment. She'd much prefer to stay and learn more about Lacy than to accompany Mrs. Steele to the catacombs.

MRS. STEELE *(turning to the others)*: No one should fraternize with Miss Brink or engage her in any discussion. She needs to realize that even if we have to accept her officially, we don't have to do it willingly. And as for tea, I'm quite sure there is nothing in the rules saying that we have to serve her.

During this little speech, Raven, who is perched on the monument behind Mrs. Steele, does a perfect imitation of the facial expressions and hand gestures of the cantankerous woman. It is hilarious, but no one dares to even crack a smile.

Lacy is astonished and immediately falls in love with the impudent bird.

Satisfied that her point has been made, Mrs. Steele is about to leave when she notices Lacy's jacket on the ground.

MRS. STEELE: See? She doesn't even put away her things. No manners whatsoever.

SAM *(quickly picks up the jacket)*: She doesn't know where or *how* to put her things away yet.

He walks over to the spot by the stone bench where Lacy first appeared and drops the jacket. It falls through the dirt into Lacy's grave and disappears.

With a harrumph, Mrs. Steele turns and exits back through the catacomb entrance. Reluctantly, Maria follows.

[You may have noticed a discrepancy of style by this point, dear Reader. In my narrative bits, Mrs. Steele and Dr. Hosler are the only characters I refer to by surname and corresponding honorific. This is at their request. The other characters did not mind the more informal use of the first name.]

The moment the catacomb portal closes, Cumberland's crypt door opens and Virginia pops out. She races over to Lacy, holding up her ankle length skirt so she can move quickly. Cumberland stays halfway in the crypt and peers out with nervous curiosity.

VIRGINIA *(looking Lacy over and speaking in a hushed whisper)*: A Modern in our little necropolis! Dash my wig! And look at the outfit! Is this what we're wearing now? No wonder Mrs. Steele's pantaloons are in a complete twist. Right, Sammy?

Virginia turns to Sam and notices how firmly and warmly his eyes are glued to the girl. She looks next at Cumberland and sees a look of interest in his eyes, too. For over one hundred years, Virginia has been the main object of male adoration in the cemetery, and she experiences a stab of envy. Artfully, she takes two steps to the left, a move that effectively blocks Cumberland's view of the newcomer.

Lacy, standing alone, shifts uncomfortably, feeling Virginia's animosity. It is just my luck, she thinks, to get a mean girl in the mix.

Dr. Hosler approaches again, looking at Lacy as if he is examining a rare butterfly that has been captured and pinned to a museum wall.

DR. HOSLER: She looks as if she was well nourished, but I do wonder at the reasoning of the attire. Surely those are not the clothes one wears in public. Look at the length of the skirt. Are they burying people in their unmentionables these days?

Shyly Sarah removes her beloved lace shawl from her shoulders and demonstrates how to tie it around her waist so that it creates a kind of skirt that covers the thighs and then she quickly offers it to Lacy without making eye contact. The gesture is more than sweet. She's looking out for Lacy. Even though Lacy doesn't particularly want the shawl, she sees how hiding her thighs might help to keep Mrs. Steele off her back. She thanks Sarah and ties the shawl around her waist.

Sam notices with a slight blush that the effect is the opposite of what Mrs. Steele probably would want: the veiling of Lacy's firm thighs with the white lace only makes her look more desirable. But he keeps this to himself, and Sarah scuttles off to prepare the tea.

The other "regulars" for the customary serving of tea emerge: two old sisters—Effie and Neffie Spindly—who, even after a century, no one can tell apart. They typically sit together and embroider, as Effie was buried with her sewing basket, and because of this, no one pays them the slightest attention. Tonight Effie brings her basket as usual, but they are too curious to sit by themselves and do needlework. Instead they tiptoe from their family crypt and join the huddle around Lacy.

EFFIE: We heard the profanity and the consequences. A new resident! Goodness gracious!

NEFFIE: Fiddlesticks. The girl should just say *fiddlesticks* or she'll get another strike.

EFFIE: Or she could just keep quiet.

NEFFIE: She should definitely mind her p's and q's.

Lacy looks from face to face, growing more uneasy.

LACY: Can I talk with you privately, Sam?

Sam blushes deeply, and all react as if she has just asked Sam to join her in robbing a bank.

VIRGINIA: Oooh, Sammy.

DR. HOSLER: It's very risky. That would definitely be fraternizing.

LACY: I don't want to cause trouble. I just have so many questions about where I am . . . how it all works. The rules came at me so fast.

Sam thinks. He wants to help her, but he can't afford to upset Mrs. Steele. Perhaps they could give her information without actually talking to her.

SAM *(to the other residents but clearly intending for Lacy to hear)*: I have a thought. While we are having our tea, the new resident may ask a question or two aloud, not because she expects us to converse with her, but because she is talking to herself. And if we hear such questions, we might discuss the answers with one another, and if she happens to hear the answers, that is not our fault.

There is a beat of silence as the others understand what Sam is suggesting.

DR. HOSLER: Excellent idea.

Lacy nods and sits on the stone bench, grateful not only for Sam's willingness to help, but also for his gathering of support for her.

Dr. Hosler removes his top hat, and he and the Spindly sisters sit in their usual places for tea: on thick, squat tombstones evenly placed around a sarcophagus, the flat surface of which is table-height, not too far from Lacy's bench.

Virginia ordinarily doesn't bother to come up for tea, and she doesn't particularly want to help Lacy, but she can't possibly miss out on something new. She sits where Maria usually sits, at the foot of the stone coffin.

Cumberland plays it safe and stays close to his crypt, but he makes sure, for Lacy's benefit, to pose in what he thinks of as an attractive manner: hands on his hips, one foot up on a low tombstone.

Sam perches where he usually does, which is on the sloped, waist-high roof of the Watson crypt next to the Poe monument. He doesn't particularly like his own tombstone, which is in a depressing section way in the back.

Sarah emerges from the same crypt with a tray bearing a pretty china teapot and matching cups. *[Although the Watsons are not allowed out anymore, they are kind enough to allow Sarah to borrow their tea set. You'll learn more about this soon, dear Reader.]* Sarah walks around the table, serving tea to everyone except Lacy, the supposed *persona non grata*, to whom she gives an embarrassed and apologetic smile.

Sam nods at Lacy to begin the charade of sorts.

LACY: Okay . . . I'm just going to talk out loud over here, and I know nobody is going to talk directly back. I have so many questions. I don't know where to start . . . um . . . okay . . . this whole strike thing. I know that I don't want to get three strikes, but I'm not sure what it all means . . . I heard something about privileges.

There is a beat of silence as the group takes in Lacy's question. They sip their tea and glance at one another cautiously, uncertain how to begin. Finally Sam starts, and as they converse, they pretend as if Lacy isn't there.

SAM *(looking at Dr. Hosler)*: When I was a new resident, it took me a while to understand what "aboveground privileges" meant. Was that true for you, too, Doctor?

DR. HOSLER: Yes. I didn't realize at first that the Dead are allowed to rise every evening at or after midnight to enjoy appropriate recreation—

VIRGINIA: Meaning boring recreation—

DR. HOSLER: As long as one is back in the grave before the sun rises.

CUMBERLAND: And as long as one does not have three strikes.

Virginia can see that Cumberland is hoping that Lacy is noticing him, and this irritates her even further.

NEFFIE: Three strikes and you become one of the Suppressed, which means you lose your aboveground privileges. Isn't that correct, Sister?

EFFIE: True.

A sad voice comes from a grave to Lacy's left, which is marked Clarissa Smythe, 1852–1869.

CLARISSA *(remaining unseen underground)*: That means you have to lie in your grave every single night and do nothing but listen to the goings-on above.

At the sound of Clarissa's voice, Owen rises slowly and even the air seems to cringe. Just as he did earlier with the other offenders, he walks heavily toward Clarissa's grave, but something about the energy that comes from his footsteps makes Lacy summon her courage to look, to really look, at him. Although his hulk of a body is rolling forward like a great wheel of stone, a particular kind of deep sorrow shines in his eyes, the kind of sorrow that comes when the heart is breaking and the love inside pours up through a crack. He is a sweet, soulful boy, Lacy realizes. He hates his job, and suppressing seventeen-year-old Clarissa Smythe is the last thing he wants to do. He must be in love with her, Lacy guesses. Lacy glances around, wondering if others see what she sees in Owen, and there is Sam, sitting cross-legged on the roof of the Watson crypt, cap in his hands, with a look of sympathy on his face for Owen that warms her heart and makes a funny lump rise in Lacy's throat.

SARAH *(whispering sweetly)*: Hush now, Clarissa. Go back to sleep.

CLARISSA: I won't say another word. I'm sorry, Owen.

There is silence. Owen stares at her grave for a moment, grateful and sad, and then slowly returns to his seat by the wall. Lacy gets up and looks at the grass in front of Clarissa's crumbling tombstone. She can't see Clarissa, but she can imagine her lying there.

LACY: This is all wrong. It shouldn't be like this.

There is another silence. Lacy has said a truth that none of them likes to think about.

EFFIE *(leans in and whispers to the others in a sudden confession)*: I remember being afraid of the Suppressed at first. I thought they must be terrible people.

NEFFIE: Me, too. But when I started seeing lovely people like Clarissa and the Watsons get their strikes, I realized they're just like the rest of us.

Lacy looks at Owen, who has resumed his motionless position.

LACY: Who exactly is he?

At that, the others look at Owen, but he doesn't react.

SAM *(lowering his voice even more)*: If a new resident were to wonder about Owen Hapliss, I would explain that the Suppressed are not allowed to make noise or try to fraternize or scream or cry out or try to escape. If one does, Owen Hapliss has to keep the individual from rising. He's the Suppressor. That's his job.

Owen's gaze is down, his broad shoulders slumped, looking as beaten as the iron he used to forge. Although he is a terrifying figure, Lacy wants to get up and put her arms around him.

LACY: If you are Suppressed, how long do you have to stay down there? Not . . . forever?

There is a long pause. It's a difficult question. Finally Sam speaks.

SAM: I would explain to a new resident that . . . that . . .
VIRGINIA *(impatiently)*: The Suppressed don't have a chance to be liberated. There. I said it.
EFFIE: Virginia!
VIRGINIA: It's true.
NEFFIE *(whispering)*: We don't know that for certain.
DR. HOSLER: I would explain to a new resident that none of us knows the answer to the bigger question of whether this reality is what one might call the end. Many believe this is merely a waiting room of sorts, although we have no evidence one way or the other.

EFFIE: I believe there is a better place.

NEFFIE: I believe those of us who aren't Suppressed will get to go to a better place, which is why I don't take any chances on getting any strikes.

EFFIE: I respectfully differ with my sister's opinion. I believe there might be hope for the Suppressed. Maybe a second chance in another place.

Owen looks up, hopeful for Clarissa's sake.

There is a beat of silence, and then Sarah speaks up in a quiet voice.

SARAH: I was promised Heaven.

A tired melancholy settles over the collective as each individual recalls the disappointment they felt upon finding themselves in the reality in which they now reside.

EFFIE: It's still a possibility!

VIRGINIA: Unlikely.

DR. HOSLER: In the meantime, we carry on the best we can, don't we?

NEFFIE *(whispering)*: I would tell a new resident to try and avoid the wrath of Mrs. Steele.

VIRGINIA *(rising and walking over to stand next to Cumberland)*: I would tell a new resident to keep to herself as much as possible.

Virginia gives Lacy a cold, stay-away-from-my-man smile. She reminds Lacy of Rachel Catrin, a girl in high school who would say she's trying to be helpful while she pushed you off a cliff. First, Lacy has no interest in Cumberland Poltroon; and second, that kind of competitive, paranoid jealousy is the last thing Lacy needs.

Shaking off the unnecessary hostility, Lacy gets up and begins to pace, thinking out loud about what her afterlife here is going to be like.

LACY: So here's what I have learned so far. I'm in some kind of seriously old-fashioned realm of existence, which may or may not lead to a better place, and I have to follow ridiculous rules, like saying *fiddlesticks*, which is harder than you think. I mean, things have changed as far as language goes. The f-word is as common as shi—See, that's what I mean. Trying not to break this one little rule is going to take a hel—sinki amount of concentration, but I have to succeed because if I get three strikes, then I become a buried-alive dead person instead of just a dead person, which I definitely don't want to be. And if by some miracle I don't become Suppressed, then I get to come out every night at midnight and enjoy a fu—ndamental cup of tea . . . that's the big reward, right?

The table is silent. Finally it's Virginia who breaks the silence.

VIRGINIA: Well done. You've grasped the situation in all its glory.

Lacy understands and even appreciates the bitterness in Virginia's voice. Virginia tells it like it is. She and Virginia are more alike than she realized.

EFFIE *(to Virginia)*: Dear, remember we're supposed to be talking to one another, not to her.

There is an awkward pause, which Sarah tries to shorten by pouring another round of tea. Lacy looks at the teapot and the teacups.

LACY: Wait a minute . . . we can drink? Can we eat? How does that work?

Although Sarah is shy, she feels it is her duty to speak.

SARAH: As President of the Food and Drink Committee, I'd explain to a new resident that ethereal food and drink are permitted. Except, of course, Mrs. Steele doesn't allow alcohol.

DR. HOSLER: Which is ridiculous since it has no effect on us.

EFFIE: Of course, we can't drink or eat the food of the Living, and, technically, we don't need anything at all. But people like going through the motions.

LACY *(blurts)*: You mean it's not really tea?

SAM *(jumps in)*: A new resident might wonder if the tea is really tea, and I would explain that it's *ethereal* tea. It's made of ether instead of water.

NEFFIE: Lovely flavor.

VIRGINIA: If you like the taste of air.

DR. HOSLER: I remember how hard it was to grasp at first, but the worlds of the Living and the Dead are made of entirely different matter. We, the Deceased, cannot hold or manipulate anything of the world of the Living. For example, we can't cut down these trees or throw a rock through that church window or open the gate.

Lacy notices an empty bottle of vodka that someone has left by the church wall. She goes to pick it up and can't. And then she realizes something that has been bothering her subconsciously all along. It is autumn and the grounds are strewn with fallen leaves, yet there is no rustling or crunching of the leaves beneath her footsteps when she walks.

SAM: Similarly, we cannot be heard or seen by the Living. They can't feel us if we touch them.

DR. HOSLER: We do, however, have the power to manipulate things of our own world, and what counts as "things of our own world" are our graves, crypts, and sarcophagi, and anything in them, our own bodies, our clothing, the items that have been buried with us, et cetera. These things go through a physical transformation that I cannot explain and become made of the kind of matter that we, the Dead, are made of.

NEFFIE: The reason we have some items that we can use is because these items were buried with us.

SAM: Lucky for me, one of my fellow soldiers came to my funeral with this *(he lifts the leather satchel he wears across his chest)* and put it into my coffin, so now I have my pencil, my knife, and my journal at my eternal disposal. I'm forever grateful.

DR. HOSLER: My top hat and medical bag are other examples. *(He tips his hat and holds up his bag.)* I taught many a student the art of surgery with the tools in this bag.

Lacy recalls the shock of his knife sliding into her heart and shudders.

NEFFIE: My sister was buried with her sewing kit. So we have a needle, thread, and several lovely handkerchiefs to embroider.

The sisters hold up their handkerchiefs, every inch of them covered with delicate stitches.

VIRGINIA *(dryly)*: I was buried with a poem. Lot of good that did me.

From Sarah's expression, Lacy can see that she would have appreciated a poem. Sarah catches Lacy looking at her and quickly diverts the attention by pouring more tea.

SARAH: This tea set was buried with Mrs. Watson in 1899.

EFFIE: Because we have so little matter in our world, most of our residents are willing to share what they have.

Lacy looks down at the lace shawl Sarah loaned her and realizes how generous it was for her to share it.

From inside the crypt marked Watson, which is where Sam is perched, a voice calls out . . .

AGNES WATSON: I'm happy to hear you're still enjoying the tea set. It was an extravagant act on the part of my dear husband to bury me with such valuable items. Most people are selfish and want to keep or sell the belongings of the departed, but he knew how much I loved that tea set and wanted me to have it in paradise.

Another voice calls out from the same crypt.

ALFRED WATSON: It was the least I could do. I wanted to imagine you having tea with the angels, darling.
AGNES WATSON: Although it didn't quite turn out that way, did it?
ALFRED WATSON: No, it didn't. Not yet, anyway.
AGNES WATSON: How is the tea tonight, Sarah dear?

During the Watsons' comments, Owen dutifully rises from his spot and walks toward the crypt. Although the leaves do not crunch under his feet, the footsteps of the Dead can be felt by other residents if they are heavy enough, and Owen's steps send booming vibrations through the earth, which Lacy feels right through the soles of her own boots.

AGNES WATSON: I feel you coming, Owen. I'm sorry. I'll be quiet.
ALFRED WATSON: Right-o. No need for a Suppression, Owen. I'm buttoning up the lips right now.

Owen returns to his post.

EFFIE: I miss the Watsons. Such a lovely couple.
NEFFIE: Quite.

The voices of the Watsons make Lacy wonder about the other souls buried here. Lacy walks around the cemetery, silently reading the names on the crowded tombstones and crypts.

LACY: Are you guys it? The only ones who aren't Suppressed?

SAM *(careful to look at the others and not at Lacy when he speaks)*: Here's a fact you might not know. Out of the 178 residents at Westminster, ten of us rise on a regular basis, 130 are Suppressed, and the other thirty-eight choose to sleep.

LACY: Choose to sleep?

EFFIE: There's not much to do up here. Is there, Neffie?

NEFFIE: If you get frustrated or angry or depressed, you run the risk of getting strikes. Because of that, I do believe that many people find that it is safer to stay asleep. Don't you agree, Effie?

LACY: Stay asleep all day and all night? How is that possible? I'd go insane.

VIRGINIA: I would, too, frankly.

DR. HOSLER *(to the sisters)*: We do have a lot of Sleepers. They hear the midnight chimes and tell themselves to go back to sleep. It's not that hard. But like those here at the table, I prefer to rise.

The others nod. Lacy looks at the collection of residents sitting around the sarcophagus with their teacups. This group represents the risk takers? It would be funny if it weren't so sad.

LACY: So, the best I can hope for is either to sleep or to drink ethereal tea and be constantly worried about breaking a rule every night for possibly all of eternity?

The residents look at one another. Finally Virginia speaks again.

VIRGINIA: An accurate summary.

LACY: Oh my Go—I'm already going crazy and I just got here. You guys have been here for over a century.

Lacy continues her walk, telling herself that there must be a way out, when a tombstone toward the back catches her eye. She walks over to read the inscription.

LACY: Samuel Henry Steele. 1848–1865. Beloved son. Brave soldier and hero who died in the Civil War.

The cemetery is small enough that Sam and the others can see and hear. Embarrassed, Sam hops off the crypt on which he was sitting and walks toward her.

SAM: You don't have to read that.
LACY: It's yours?

Lacy notices the tombstone next to Sam's is marked Gertrude Parsons Steele.

LACY *(reading)*: Gertrude Parsons Steele. 1819–1898. Beloved wife and mother, virtuous, honorable, generous, and kind. Forever loved. Forever remembered. Forever leading the way to righteousness.

Still perched on Poe's monument, Raven leans over and points the tip of a wing feather into his beak as if he is gagging.

LACY *(turning around to look at Sam)*: Oh my Go—sh. Mrs. Steele is . . .

SAM: My mother.

Raven starts whistling Berlioz's "March to the Scaffold." The Spindly sisters giggle.

VIRGINIA *(cuttingly)*: Of course, if you're related to Mrs. Steele, you may not have to worry as much as the rest of us.

A current of discomfort runs through the company, and Sam turns gray. Virginia has alluded to something about which none of them has ever spoken: twice Sam has deserved a third strike—once for profanity and once for taking off his jacket and trying to rip it in half—and Mrs. Steele conveniently didn't hear or see either transgression. Although not in Sam's control, these oversights on the part of Mrs. Steele bred an edge of ill will toward Sam, even from those who essentially sympathize with him. Since then, Sam has walked the line with extra caution, afraid to break a rule lest his mother show him any more favoritism.

Although Lacy does not know this backstory, she can feel the tension and guess the problem. Lacy's best friend in elementary school was the son of the school's principal, and she remembers how mercilessly he was teased about it. Sam has the worst of both worlds, she can see. Not only did he have to put up with having Mrs. Steele as a mother in life; he is stuck with her in the afterlife.

Lacy tries to give Sam a sympathetic smile, but he is staring at the ground. She looks down, too, and another grave catches her eye, marked HENRY JONATHAN STEELE.

LACY: Is that your dad?

SAM: I don't remember much. He died when I was young. He chooses to sleep.

I don't fucking blame him, Lacy thinks.

EFFIE *(calls out to him in a loud whisper)*: Samuel, I think that's fraternizing.

Embarrassed, Sam quickly turns away from Lacy, hurries back, and climbs up to his perch on the Watson crypt.

Lacy looks at the group, all of whom quickly resume drinking their tea. Each of them looks lonely and sad. Virginia doesn't love Cumberland. Lacy can tell. She's just using him to keep from being bored to death. Cumberland hates himself for his cowardice. Lacy sees it in his eyes, even though he tries to pose like a stud. Dr. Hosler is dying for stimulation and misses teaching. Poor Owen, forever on duty and off to the side, is suffering from forbidden love. At least the Spindly sisters have each other and their embroidery, but the way they sit on the edges of their seats . . . they clearly crave more excitement. And then there's Sam.

Lacy watches Sam pull out his journal to write something down and the way he's sitting, hunched over, legs crossed, melts her. If it weren't for his dated uniform, he could be a friend of hers from school, and this makes her imagine the two of them together. Quite naturally, she imagines them in scenes from her former world. There they are talking and eating at Crimmson's Café. There they are walking through Druid Hill Park and around the

Inner Harbor. There they are at her favorite bookshop. There they are at Tenuto's, getting ready to perform at the open mic, holding hands under the table to give each other encouragement.

From there her imagination takes her home and she can see herself sitting just like Sam is now, except on her own bed. It's late and she's about to fall asleep, but she wants to capture the night in her journal, so she props her three pillows behind her back and pulls her blue-and-purple quilt over her lap and she writes. She stops every now and then to look at the curtainless window with its slice of the moonlit sky and her lyrics and poems that are taped all around the windowsill.

Her sister Olivia is there, too, in her own bed behind the batik print cloth that they suspended from the ceiling two years ago to divide the room. Olivia's bedside light is on and the lamp is glowing orange through the colorful cloth. Although she and Olivia fight, Lacy likes it best when Olivia is there at night, on the other side of the curtain. Olivia is quick to laugh—especially when she is reading or scrolling through the messages on her cell phone. Lacy doesn't need to see what makes her laugh. She just likes the sound of it.

Below them both is the sound of their mother playing the keyboard with her headphones on. She has a habit of playing before bedtime, says it relaxes her after spending all day dealing with crap at work and then grading her students' problems at night. Although the keyboard speakers are turned off and Lacy and Olivia can't hear the notes, they can still hear the sound of their mom's fingers against the keys. She has been playing slowly, which she always does at first, but now the light tapping is getting stronger and faster. She's switching from whatever calm melody she was playing to a pounding thing of her own invention. Some inner beat is taking over and she's starting to really hammer out a rhythm. Lacy stops writing in her journal and looks up. She knows what's coming next.

And there it is . . . as the pounding grows louder and faster, the crooning starts: their mom's wild and strange humming that bubbles up from somewhere deep inside her soul and that she assumes no one else can hear.

As the humming grows louder and more dramatic, Olivia lifts up the curtain and rolls her eyes. "There she goes again!" She drops the curtain and Lacy laughs. It's their secret, and although they pretend it's annoying, they would never tell their mom for fear that she would stop.

Lacy laughs again and lifts the curtain to say something back to Olivia, but her hand moves through the air and she blinks and sees a bleak, gray tombstone instead. She turns, and the full view of the cemetery comes over her like a wave at the same time the memories of her warm bedroom rush out and away. Grief pulls her to her knees.

Sam and the others look.

Her eyes are wide and frightened and flooding. Her lip trembles, and as she looks helplessly at Sam, she lifts her empty hands, and it is as if everyone can see that in them she is somehow holding up the enormity of her loss. Everything she loves has floated away. Death has stranded her, has stranded all of them. Sorrow rings out from her silently, like a sound that is so intense it can only be felt.

LACY: I want to go home.

The sound of her sadness hits Sam and the others hard. It seeps into the earth and hits the Suppressed and the Sleeping, too, and all of their souls vibrate. They are pulled into their own dark wells of grief, but they are also pulled together in one well of empathy.

No one speaks or moves. Lacy starts to cry. At the sound, Sam looks back up. Her face is raw and real. He wants to comfort her, but he remains still. Lacy can feel Sam's spirit reaching for her and yet restraining itself, and the fact that her new friend has to hold back turns the wave of grief inside her into something sharp that seems to cut her throat. She tries to keep still, but her body rocks forward and she sobs. Ethereal tears, she notices, aren't wet. They gather in her eyes and when she blinks she can feel them rolling down her cheeks, but they're unlike any substance she has ever felt, like tiny, silk-filled drops of air. She sobs louder. The sound is naked and quiet and human and unbearable.

They want to cry, too, every single one of them, for everything and everyone that they have lost, for everything and everyone they still miss, but the old habits push them forward and they mistakenly do what most well-meaning people do: they distract attention from the gaping wound with flimsy, irrelevant words. Paradoxically, it's those who commiserate the most with Lacy who are the first to speak. Their voices are fragile and tentative. They don't mean to minimize Lacy's feelings. They just don't know what else to do.

SARAH: More tea, anyone?
EFFIE: Thank you. I'm still half full, dear.
NEFFIE: I'll take a spot.

DR. HOSLER: Look at that. The moon is almost full.

They all look up, as if gazing at the moon will give Lacy the privacy she needs to pull herself together.

Cumberland gives Virginia a half-hearted nod and retires into his crypt; Sarah pours Neffie's tea.

Instinctively Lacy drags the back of her hand across her tear-drenched face, although her hand doesn't dampen. Sam cannot stand to see her like this, on her knees, crying. Longing to say something that might bring her some measure of comfort, he slides off the Watson crypt and approaches her. He speaks into his cap, which he holds in his hands, because he is afraid that he will break down if he looks into her eyes.

SAM *(whispering)*: Westminster is a quiet place to write poetry. I'm just saying that because I thought I heard a mention of poetry earlier . . . As long as you don't get that third strike, you can stay here with me . . . Not *with* me. You can stay here *like* me . . . That's what I meant. You can stay here like me and write poems. I'm not saying that I'm a poet or anything, I'm just—

Sam stops. He is a failure. He doesn't know how to talk or what to say. He is about to apologize when Raven suddenly flaps his wings in a warning. The residents freeze as Mrs. Steele and Maria emerge from the catacomb portal.

On Maria's face is a look of pity. On Mrs. Steele's is a smirk. Mrs. Steele claps her hands and calls out.

MRS. STEELE: Gather around, everyone. Mrs. Clemm has an important announcement to make.

SCENE 4: JOB ASSIGNMENT

It has been decades since there were announcements to be made at Westminster Cemetery. Now, Mrs. Steele takes a position on the front steps of the church and pulls Maria up to join her so that she can be seen and heard—hardly necessary given the small size of the cemetery and the even smaller size of the crowd. It's just the regulars—Sam, Sarah, Dr. Hosler, Virginia, and the Spindly sisters—who gather, standing at the foot of the steps. Cumberland doesn't venture out of his crypt. Owen remains sitting in his usual position on the side, although he is not noticed. Raven, perched on Poe's monument, can see and hear it all.

Dreading whatever is coming next and hesitant to join the group, Lacy takes a seat on a tombstone, which is a dozen paces or so away from the front steps of the church. But then she catches Sam's eye for just a moment and he changes his position, stepping farther from his mother and closer to her, and that little act of solidarity gives her the strength to stand and face the women.

Mrs. Steele scowls at Lacy and turns to Maria.

MRS. STEELE: Go right ahead with your announcement, Mrs. Clemm.

MARIA *(looking as if she wants to crawl under a large rock)*: As President of the Committee to Assign Committee Assignments, it is my duty to inform Miss Lacy Brink that she will be . . . President of the Termite Collection Committee.

There is a collective gasp. Sam, Sarah, Dr. Hosler, and the Spindly sisters all turn and give Lacy sympathetic glances. Even Virginia winces.

MRS. STEELE *(smiles)*: I think the job will be inspirational. She should get started right away.

SAM: What about letting her sing the Welcome Song? That would be a good job—

MRS. STEELE: Shh! We have chosen a job that needs to be filled.

LACY: What is the job exactly? Or is no one allowed to talk to me?

MRS. STEELE: The President of the Termite Collection Committee goes from grave to grave every night collecting and disposing of any termites that have entered into the wooden coffins of the residents. Our coffins are our beds. We don't like them to disintegrate. For those of us in more permanent structures—such as caskets made from cement or stone—it is not so much of a worry. But those of us in wooden coffins are often plagued with termite infestations.

At this, an arm pops straight up out of a grave marked Mariah Johnson. Lacy can tell by the white lace sleeve and the elegant glove that the resident is—or was—rich. Her hand is cupped and Lacy can guess what she's holding.

LACY: But I thought the Dead couldn't touch anything of the Living. Wouldn't that include termites?

DR. HOSLER: Termites enter inside our coffins and so become part of our world. Remember that whatever is inside our coffin goes through a transformation process.

Lacy walks over and looks into Mariah's cupped palm. A handful of translucent larvae roil and wriggle. Lacy's stomach turns. Mrs. Steele has deliberately found the most disgusting job for her and forced Maria to assign it, no doubt in an effort to make Lacy so frustrated she will scream and get her third strike. More arms with cupped hands pop up.

Determined not to let this woman win, Lacy brushes the termites from Mariah's palm into her own and then turns and smiles at Mrs. Steele.

LACY: I'm not afraid of a few bugs. What do I do with them?

MRS. STEELE *(smiles)*: You eat them.

Horrified, Lacy drops the bugs.

LACY: What the hel—*(she catches herself)*—lo.

Sam runs to her side and starts collecting the termites before they can crawl back into the earth.

LACY *(whispers to Sam)*: Can't I just toss them over the gate?

MRS. STEELE: We have found that eating them is the most effective way of making them disappear.

DR. HOSLER *(shrugs)*: It's true. If we throw them over, they just come back. Eating them seems to decommission them for good.

EFFIE: Mr. Hirston was our last termite-collection president, wasn't he?

NEFFIE: He didn't last long, if I recall. Wasn't he Suppressed for disorderly hysterics after just three nights?

SAM *(making a futile plea to his mother)*: We have been getting along without anybody in that role for a long time, ma'am. People have been eating their own. I don't mind eating them.

Sam pops the termites he had picked from the ground into his mouth.

MRS. STEELE: Samuel!

As Mrs. Steele pulls Sam aside to give him a lecture, more extended arms appear. Lacy feels anger rise, but she takes a breath. The fucking bugs are not even real, she tells herself. They're ghost bugs. All she needs to do is swallow them. If Sam can do it, she can do it. She walks over to another raised hand and takes one termite.

Sam and his mother turn to watch. There's a rule, although Lacy can't remember the number, about no job-related complaining. Lacy tosses the bug into her mouth and almost gags. She forces it down and gives Mrs. Steele a defiant look.

LACY: Delicious.

MRS. STEELE: Only a few hundred termites to go.

LACY: No problem.

As she speaks, Lacy walks from resident to resident, brushing the termites from their palms into the shawl she is wearing like a skirt. Raven whistles a tune that sounds suspiciously like "Eating Goober Peas."

LACY: I'm going to collect them all and enjoy them one at a time. Like popcorn. Except gummier. I'll eat them and read over the two million rules I'm supposed to know.

Lacy dumps all the bugs onto the stone bench, smiles fiercely at Mrs. Steele, walks over to Sam, and puts out her hand for the scroll of rules. Since she is blocking him from Mrs. Steele's view, Sam can afford an admiring smile. He hands her the scroll, which she takes over to the bench. She sits down and begins to read, popping another termite in her mouth and forcing herself to swallow it.

Mrs. Steele scowls and sits down in her usual place for tea. Sarah hurries to serve her.

LACY: Anyone who wants to can sit and watch me eat and read all night long. It will be very entertaining.

Lacy pops another termite into her mouth.

In silence the residents resume their positions around the tea table, Sam hopping up on the Watson crypt. Now that Mrs. Steele is ensconced, they pretend indifference toward Lacy, which Lacy understands. The best way for her to get and keep allies is to make sure that nobody gets in trouble because of her. Knowing that Mrs. Steele is scrutinizing her over every sip of her tea, Lacy braces herself and eats another termite as she unwinds more of the scroll.

After the first ten Rules of Etiquette, which she knows are the most important, the rules are a haphazard collection, some of which serve as explanations, while others beg questions.

Rule 19: No currency exists in the afterlife; as such the Deceased are relieved from all need to earn money.

That makes sense.

Rule 20: Since Deceased Children progress without appearing in the cemetery system, Deceased Parents are relieved of any and all parental duties.

Lacy looks around. She hasn't seen any little kids, although she remembers seeing kids' tombstones. What does that mean? Where are they? What does "progress" even mean?

Rule 21: Living animals cannot see or communicate with the Dead with the exception of ravens and black cats.

Lacy looks up at the Poe monument. Raven waves.

The handwriting in the scroll is difficult to read and, after a while, she finds that her mind is wandering. West Fayette Street is quiet. It must be two in the morning. Or later? What day is it? It's as if all the numbers have jumped off the calendars and clocks and have dissipated like the fog.

Through the iron gate to the left, the stoplight at the corner is visible. Lacy watches it turn from yellow to red, although no car is there to stop. She imagines a car racing through, thinking no one was watching. Do people run red lights in the dead of night? She sees the road as if she is in the passenger seat and the car is speeding through the intersection . . . A queasy feeling creeps into her stomach and she turns her focus away. A light in a top-floor apartment flicks on and then off.

She imagines a woman walking out of the building and across the street, imagines her standing right there, hands on the gate, imagines trying to talk to the woman and watching her remain unresponsive.

It's so odd to see the familiar sights of the Living World and yet know that she is separate.

How did this happen? How could this have happened? Again, she tries to remember the night. A police siren wails in the distance, and it dawns on her for the first time that what happened to her might not have been an accident. A chill runs through her and she turns instinctively to Sam and lets her thoughts out in a rush.

LACY: What if I was robbed and murdered? Maybe that's why I don't have my phone. My mom was on me all the time not to walk at night. She was always showing me stuff she heard on the news about people getting robbed and raped and beat up and killed. Maybe I was walking to the open mic at Tenuto's and somebody followed me and when I stopped in here some son of a bi—lly goat killed me! *(She gets up.)* I should be allowed to find him, right? I mean, at the very least I can haunt him, right? Isn't that the way it works?

She looks up at Sam on the crypt. With Mrs. Steele right there, he doesn't dare answer her directly. The other residents are equally afraid to help. Sam quickly makes a job of brushing nonexistent dirt off one of his boots and finally turns to Dr. Hosler and plays the same game they were playing before.

SAM: I remember when I died, I was surprised to find out that we can't do anything in the world of the Living. The Living can't hear us or see us or feel us and so all those ghost stories about spirits knocking on walls and creaking about in attics and blowing curtains and extinguishing lights . . . those aren't true.

DR. HOSLER: Yes, Samuel. Even if a murdered resident could find out who murdered her—or him—and even if that resident could physically leave Westminster, she—or he—couldn't do anything of any consequence to that murderer.

Mrs. Steele scowls. She sees through them, but they are breaking no rules.

LACY: This is ridiculous. There has to be justice, right? So what are we supposed to do . . . just accept the fact that we can't do a fu—

Mrs. Steele is leaning forward, eagerly watching Lacy grow more and more impassioned. With an aggravated sigh, Lacy shuts up and sits back down. She won't do herself any favors by getting another strike. With a barely audible growl, she returns to reading the scroll and forces another bug down her throat.

The night passes slowly. When it's clear no one is drinking more tea, Sarah collects the set, returns it to the Watson crypt, bids a good night, and descends to her grave. Dr. Hosler, the Spindly sisters, and Maria give up and retreat to their graves. Although they would like to offer a word of condolence or at least a "good night" to Lacy, no one dares. Virginia lasts another half hour and then gives Mrs. Steele her sweetest smile and retires as well.

Now it is just Sam, Mrs. Steele, and the ever-present Owen, whose job requires him to rise at midnight and remain vigilant until daybreak.

As Owen sits motionless and Sam writes in his journal, Mrs. Steele dozes off and then wakes with a start. When she dozes off again, Sam hops off the crypt. He passes by Lacy's bench, silently snatches a handful of termites, eats them, and returns to his seat. Lacy catches his eye and mouths, "Thank you, Sam."

Thus begins a game that gets the two through the night. Whenever Mrs. Steele dozes off, Sam makes another round and reduces Lacy's pile of termites by another handful. Raven nods at Sam with what looks like respect, and Lacy sneaks Sam as many secret glances of gratitude as possible.

After a while, the pile is gone and the rules have been read. Although Lacy has no way of marking it, she can sense that it must be near morning.

She is right. After another moment or two, a door of earth in front of the grave marked Peter Brown opens and out steps a handsome young man, not much older than his wife Sarah, shy in appearance and slight in build. Having grown up in a family of oystermen and yet plagued by seasickness, Peter had been responsible for selling rather than dredging. Every day since he was a boy, he worked the Fells Point market calling out, "Fine, fresh oysters! Cool, smooth meat! The meatiest to eat!" Here at Westminster, Peter is the Town Crier, whose primary job is to warn residents of daybreak. Like most of the others, he chooses to stay asleep much of the time, not wanting to take a chance at getting his third strike. Although he and Sarah are kind to each other, they aren't at all close—something Lacy will notice.

Like most of the unseen others, Peter listened in on much of the conversation tonight, enough to know about the unorthodox new resident, Lacy Brink. Now, he uses his job as his excuse to get a peek at the newcomer.

Lacy returns his glance with curiosity of her own, not knowing anything about his job, assuming he is just another gawker. She is wondering if she should wave or not when he pulls a bell from his waistband, stands straight, and rings the bell twice. His voice is crystal clear and loud enough to make Lacy jump.

PETER: Oyez! Oyez! Five minutes till daybreak.

He rings his bell and begins his route, which is to walk twice around the property, clockwise, a job that he is supposed to do regardless of whether anyone is up.

LACY: Oh yeah. I read about this. Residents will be given fair warning of daybreak each and every night. *(To Peter)* You must be the Town Crier. I'm Lacy Brink.

Peter gives her a quick glance but keeps going. Owen rises and, without looking at anyone, returns to his grave. Happy to see Peter and Owen complying with her request to ignore the girl, Mrs. Steele stands and smooths her skirt. She walks over to the stone bench for an inspection, notices that the termites have all been eaten, and exhales sharply. She takes the scroll from Lacy and hands it back to Sam.

MRS. STEELE: Well, it seems that the night has passed. Rest well, Samuel. I will see you tomorrow. *(She walks over to her grave and a door of earth opens. She turns back and smiles at Sam.)* Perhaps the new girl will decide to stay up.

The color drains from Sam's face and he wants to turn and remind Lacy of the rule, but she is a step ahead.

LACY *(to Mrs. Steele)*: I'm not an idiot. I know I have to be in bed before the sun rises.

Lacy fakes a gigantic yawn. Mrs. Steele gives her one last scowl, descends into her grave, and shuts the door.

Sam breathes a sigh of relief.

They share a smile and then Lacy looks down nervously at the spot where Sam had said she was buried.

LACY: How does this work? I don't think I really have a grave—or at least not one with a door. *(She looks at the other graves and crypts.)* And even if I did have a door, how can I open it if I can't open the gate or pick up a rock? I know there was something about this in the rules. *(She looks at the scroll, which is now in Sam's hands.)*

Sam wants desperately to defy Mrs. Steele, to run over to Lacy, to take her in his arms and tell her that he will help her through this ordeal, to tell her that he will be by her side until the end of time itself, to tell her that he will protect her and cherish her, but he answers matter-of-factly without looking at her.

SAM: Regardless of whether you've been buried or cremated, you can simply jump onto the spot and you will be instantly subsumed. But old habits die hard, and most of us enter and exit the more respectable way—through a door. We have physical sovereignty over our burial plots, which includes the doors to our crypts, coffins, sarcophagi, and catacombs. We can open and close them by merely imagining them to open and close.

To demonstrate, Sam runs over to his grave. A door of earth opens. Although there are no stair steps, per se, he moves downward by intention. He turns and comes back up, making sure that Lacy is watching. Then he closes the door and demonstrates the second method. He simply jumps onto the same spot and he instantly disappears through the ground into his grave. He hops out the same way.

Lacy's eyes are wide. She turns to look at her burial spot. She imagines a door opening, and in the next instant, a small, roughly cut lid of earth lifts and shifts to the side.

LACY: Amazing. *(She peers into the dark hole that is revealed.)* That is way too small, though, Sam. That's like the size of a basic trash can.

SAM: The size doesn't matter. Our matter fits in and out of whatever size was used for our interment.

Lacy knows he's trying to help, and she is exhausted, but she is still terrified at the thought of going underground.

SAM *(whispering)*: It's not so bad, Miss Brink. Sleep, that is. I was afraid at first, but I grew accustomed to it. And you need sleep. Sometimes you don't even realize how tired you are. Good night, Miss Brink.

He walks to his own grave, descends halfway, and then stops and turns for one more look.

Lacy stands motionless. The image of her bed reappears in her mind, the blue-and-purple quilt, the three pillows, just the way she likes it, and the wave of homesickness rises again.

PETER *(walks past, ringing his bell)*: Oyez! Oyez! Daybreak in one minute.

Peter rings one last time and descends into his grave.

Lacy turns and sees Sam, half in his grave, looking at her with concern, motioning for her to go to sleep.

Lacy *(whispering)*: I just want to go home, Sam.

Quickly Sam climbs out of his grave and rushes over.

SAM: I know, Miss Brink. I'm sorry, but it's almost sunrise.
LACY: Can't I just sleep on the bench?
SAM: The Deceased must return to the *earth* by sunrise. No exceptions.
LACY: Or what? When the sunlight touches our ghostly skin do we burst into flame? *(She is hoping that Sam will laugh, but he doesn't say anything.)* Sam, I was joking. Really . . . what happens to us?
SAM: I don't know, Miss Brink. It's one of those chances none of us dares take.
LACY *(stares at the ground)*: This is really, really scary.
SAM: Ten seconds. Good night.

Sam heads back toward his grave. From underground, the voices of the Deceased begin the ritual countdown.

VOICES OF THE DEAD: Ten, nine, eight . . .

Raven hops onto the very top of Poe's monument and settles his wings.

LACY *(whispers again)*: Sam! *(On his way to his grave, he stops and rushes back.)* Can't I sleep with you?

SAM *(blushing)*: Sleep with me?

LACY: I'm sorry . . . I don't mean *with* you. I mean next to you . . . nearby . . . in the same region.

VOICES OF THE DEAD: Seven, six, five . . .

SAM: You must sleep in your own grave. You can do it, Miss Brink.

LACY: Sam?

SAM: Yes?

LACY: Can you just call me Lacy?

SAM: I'll hold your hand, Lacy.

VOICES OF THE DEAD: Four, three . . .

LACY *(touched, she holds out her hand)*: That is so swee—

Sam pushes her into her grave. Before she has the chance to scream, she sinks out of sight. He runs and leaps into his own grave.

VOICES OF THE DEAD: Two . . . one . . .

BLACKOUT.

SCENE 5: THE LIVING

The day dawns, and we gradually see and hear the rising sights and sounds of the Living. Outside the iron gate, cars and buses begin to roll by. As the sun burns through, the colors of the scene send a little shock through us. The world of the Dead, which we have been in up until now, is washed only in white and black and gray.

We can only see what is happening on West Fayette Street through the gate. If we close our eyes, we can experience the coming day as Lacy must, through sound alone. If, as for Lacy, this is our first day underground, we will be unable to sleep and the sounds will hold us in their grip. We hear an ambulance in the far distance and the bass thump of music from a passing car. There is that crunch of dry leaves beneath footsteps that is missing from the Dead. Lacy is guessing it's a pedestrian walking down the leaf-strewn sidewalk close to the gate.

As the minutes pass and one hour leads to the next, sounds rise, merge, cross, and fade: the hum of traffic, snippets of conversations, commuters rushing to work. More footsteps, a family asking for directions to the hospital, a drunk asking for spare change, a one-sided cell phone conversation, laughter, an argument between a couple, one girl teasing another about a boy. The human voices and the fragments of conversations are achingly ordinary, people wholly absorbed in the daily flow of life, as if their physical existence in this time and place had always been and would always be.

The morning turns to afternoon. A few tourists arrive, as they do each day, to look at the Poe monument. Lacy can hear them read the historical plaques to each other. She can hear the "take a picture of me" requests. One man with a French accent makes a toast to Poe. Lacy can't see it, but he pours a shot glass of bourbon for the celebrated writer and leaves it on the base of the monument.

The sounds build to a crescendo and Lacy pictures the early evening rush hour. And then, as the noise lowers in intensity and volume, one sound emerges: that of a stroller on the leaf-covered brick path quite near to Lacy. The crunch stops and Lacy hears, as if close to her ear, the voice of a mother, singing. It's a silly song about five little pumpkins, and Lacy can hear the woman's smile in her voice. Lacy can imagine her leaning over to look into her baby's eyes as she sings, and when the mother gets to the end of the song, the baby laughs—a babble of excruciating beauty. The laugh, an ordinary sound really, a sound that is as common as a crack in the sidewalk, seems to float as if it is made of a rare element, a special kind of helium.

And then the crunching of the stroller resumes through the leaves and fades, and it is quiet.

Lacy's throat burns with a hot sheen of sadness. And then anger, like a match, strikes and she feels as if her soul has caught fire. The injustice of her predicament, the desire to find out who is responsible for her death, the foul-tasting hunger for revenge consume her for several long minutes, and then she closes her eyes. Suddenly exhausted, she begins to fall asleep.

Slowly, the Dead stir in their slumber, as they often do at this time, when the sun is setting and the earth is turning toward that final stretch to midnight. The evening noises, the audible affirmations of life, often make the Dead hum softly. It's not a hum made by the voice; it's rather the emission of a different kind of energy.

[The closest you could come to understanding what it sounds like, dear Reader, would be to listen to the burning of candles, which give off a lovely sound as well as a light, of course, but which the Living can't hear because the frequency is beyond mortal range.]

Without knowing what it is, Lacy hears the humming and, like a lullaby, it soothes her: the sound of each individual voice joining in an understated mycelium of harmony.

And then . . . although Lacy cannot see it, the color of the sunset is both ordinary and otherworldly in its rose-blue beauty, the last gasp of the gloaming, already inevitably slipping away.

When the sun is completely gone and yet the horizon still has a faint glow, young Clarissa Smythe appears—not completely, of course; she wouldn't take that chance. She looks out first and then when she is sure that no one else is up, she rises halfway, so that only her upper torso is aboveground. There she rests her elbows on the ground, puts her chin in her hands, and takes in the sight of the trees and sky as if she is taking in a huge breath. She has a round, deserving face, wide ready-to-smile eyes, and curly hair, braided and wound into a bun at the nape of her neck. Her dress, which she made herself, has a bold collar with a large bow.

After a moment, she turns her gaze toward the church wall. Owen Hapliss appears. He, too, stays in his grave, which is twenty feet from hers. Hearts pounding, the two gaze at each other and smile. It is their nightly ritual. They are both breaking the rules, but they have found that by staying half in their graves and by rising only for a few moments at this particular time of evening, the risk is at its lowest. They dare not speak, but they hum and they gaze as the cemetery grows darker.

One by one the Dead fall back asleep, and the music of their energy grows softer and then stops. Owen mouths "I love you" to Clarissa and she mouths it back. They return to their graves, and Westminster settles into itself.

[I have witnessed this scene between the unrequited lovers firsthand, dear Reader, and let me say here that you are fortunate to be one step removed by virtue of this narration. To directly feel the longing between them every night, to know that this fleeting exchange is the most they have, will test the absorbent properties of any handkerchief.]

There are a few hours until midnight, when the bell will toll and those who are able are allowed to rise. Only Raven remains awake, perched on Poe's monument.

After an hour or two passes, we make out a figure walking into the cemetery, and those fine hairs on the back of our necks quiver: a Living person . . . a young woman! It is a cold autumn evening, just dark, but the streetlamp at the entrance casts a halo of light, and we get a better glimpse of her as she passes under the light. Older than Lacy by two years, this is Olivia Brink, Lacy's sister. Her features are sharper than Lacy's. Her hair is cut in sharp layers, dyed reddish brown. Tonight she is wearing jeans and boots. No hat or gloves. Her hands are jammed into the deep pockets of her jacket, borrowed from her boyfriend. Troubling anger emanates from her. It's as if the jacket she's wearing is embedded with a thousand outward-pointing arrowheads.

From Poe's monument, Raven watches. Olivia looks up and sees him, which reminds us that the Living as well as the Dead can see Raven. Although she knows it's ridiculous, she swears the bird is observing her.

OLIVIA: Take a fucking picture. It lasts longer.

Drunk, she laughs at herself. I have come to this, she thinks: telling off birds for appearing as if they are watching me.

Feeling large-hearted, Raven decides to help by making several small, bird-like movements of his head, turning to look this way and that, as if each jab is random and brainless.

Olivia pulls a bottle of vodka from her coat pocket—the same size and brand as the empty one Lacy found earlier against the side of the church—and sits on the stone bench in front of Lacy's unmarked grave. She takes a long drink and then she talks to herself, her voice fluctuating between anger and sadness, the occasional bitter laugh betraying the fact that she has already had a lot to drink.

OLIVIA: So here I am again . . . Zane thinks I'm at home. Mom thinks I'm at Diana's. And Diana thinks I'm . . . I forgot what I texted her. *(She laughs.)* I'm doing an excellent job. Here's to me.

Olivia lifts the bottle and takes another drink. Her cell phone vibrates in her jeans pocket, and she ignores it, instead looking up at the bare black branches of the tree against the moonlit sky outside the gate.

OLIVIA *(singing)*:

Lacy Lacy wore a tutu.
She fell down and got a boo-boo,
Cried so hard that she went cuckoo.
So we put her in the zoo-zoo. *(Another laugh.)*

I was, like, seven, and you were five when I made up that song about you. God, you used to get so mad at me whenever I sang it . . . You hated getting teased, which made it so incredibly fun to tease you.

At the sound of Olivia's voice Lacy stirs, then feels the heavy and encompassing arms of sleep around her, and closes her eyes, believing that she is dreaming.

OLIVIA: Remember that one time when I sang it outside at Grandma's house, in front of those other kids? You got so mad. I ran inside and you followed me and you screamed and threw a saltshaker at me. Grandma put you in time-out. That made you even madder. You said it was unfair. I told Grandma that you took every little thing the wrong way, and Grandma sided with me. She told you to sit in the chair and think about how you needed thicker skin and you screamed, "What do I need thicker skin for? I'm not a rhinoceros!" And then you sat there, silent and shaking and pathetic. *(Olivia's voice takes on weight and is on the verge of cracking beneath it.)* God, Lace. Why were you so fucking easy to tease?

Olivia's intensity pulls at Lacy and shakes her out of her sleep. The ground shifts and Lacy rises halfway out of the earth to take in the unexpected sight of her sister sitting in front of her.

LACY: Olivia? Liv? I can't believe it . . .

Olivia tries to take another sip, but the bottle is empty. She swears, gets up, and tosses the bottle into the bush by the church wall.

Lacy is spellbound, watching; the familiar solidity of her sister's body unlocks a tiny window of memory. An image from that last night: the sound of Liv and Zane and Diana in the basement laughing at something as she was in the kitchen secretly getting ready to go to the open mic. She remembers her excitement. She was finally going to perform and nobody knew it. Their mom wasn't home; she was out on her first date, Lacy suddenly recalls, with some guy she had met online. Olivia and Lacy had helped her put together an outfit to wear. That had been fun.

With a stab, Lacy realizes how terrible that night must have been for her mother . . . did she get a call about her daughter's death when she was on her date?

Even though she knows that Olivia can't see or hear her, Lacy speaks.

LACY: God, Liv . . . what happened that night? How is Mom?

Olivia gets up and makes a slow circle around the bench. She sees the shot glass full of bourbon at the foot of Poe's grave and laughs. She walks over, picks it up, and smells it.

OLIVIA: Ha. See, this is a sign. I'd leave it for you, Lace, but I know you'd hate it. *(She downs the shot. Her phone buzzes again.)* Shut the fuck up. Nobody gets it, Lacy. I don't know if I can take it.

LACY: What is that supposed to mean? Liv?

Moving with sudden speed, Olivia walks to the iron gate. She opens it, walks through, and closes it. Lacy runs to the gate, but it won't open for her. The door to Sam's grave opens halfway and he peers out. Anxiously he calls to her in a hushed voice.

SAM *(whispering)*: Lacy, you're not allowed to be out all the way! It's not midnight yet.

LACY: Sam, it's my sister!

Sarah Brown hears and peers out next.

Lacy is about to call out for Olivia, but Olivia has already disappeared from sight.

SARAH *(whispering)*: Lacy, you mustn't be out. Come—

LACY: But my sister—

Sam wants to go to her, yet it's Sarah who takes the tremendous risk. Shy Sarah, who has been quiet and careful for the past 200 years, leaps out of her grave, runs to Lacy, puts her arm around her, and starts leading her back. Sam, still half in his grave, is stunned.

SARAH: Shh. Come back to bed, Lacy.

LACY: But my sister was just here. I swear it. I heard her . . . I saw her. *(Lacy resists. Silently, Sarah pulls Lacy toward her grave. Lacy pulls away.)* Will she be back? She has to know what happened to me. If I could just ask her . . .

SARAH: Shh . . . please.

The door to Mrs. Steele's grave opens and Raven caws a warning. Mrs. Steele rises halfway from her grave. From her vantage point, Lacy is visible, but Sarah is blocked by a crypt.

MRS. STEELE *(a look of triumph on her face)*: Lacy Brink, fully out of your grave before midnight! That is strike three!

Sam, remaining half in his grave like his mother, feels an anguished cry rise in his throat, but he holds it in. Sarah steps out from behind the crypt.

SARAH: No! It was my fault, Mrs. Steele. I was awakened by a cry and I rose, thinking it was already midnight. It was just a cat yowling, and so I immediately realized my error and turned to go back. I must have been half asleep because in my haste and panic, I tried to return here *(she points at the spot from which Lacy had emerged)*. Naturally, I frightened her right out of her grave! I was just apologizing. *(She turns to Lacy.)* As I was saying, I'm sorry for the intrusion. It won't happen again.

Lacy's body starts to shake. Mrs. Steele won't believe Sarah's story, Lacy is sure of it. Raven, perched on Poe's monument behind Mrs. Steele, turns his head and mimics the sound of a cat, throwing his voice to the far edge of the cemetery. When Mrs. Steele turns around to look, he tucks his head under one wing as if he has been sleeping all along. Sam finally gets the nerve to speak.

SAM: Yes! The cat woke Sarah and it woke me too, Mother. I saw the whole thing just as Sarah described it. I was clarifying how it works. *(To Lacy)* Rule 240 says that if you are roused during evening hours, you may be excused for reflexively peering out—

MRS. STEELE: But you are subject to a strike if you fully exit your grave. Sarah, you know that.

SARAH: I'm sorry.

MRS. STEELE: Look at Samuel and me. We did the right thing. Well done, Samuel.

Sam is mortified. His mother's praise only highlights his lack of courage.

SARAH: I understand if you feel that you have to give me a strike. But Lacy should not be given a strike because my arrival pushed her out.

SAM: That's right! Rule 242: If one resident tries to occupy the grave of another and the grave's owner rises to defend his or her rightful place—

MRS. STEELE *(snaps)*: I know the rule.

Lacy, Sarah, and Sam are on edge as Mrs. Steele deliberates in silence.

LACY: I—

MRS. STEELE: Quiet! *(To Sarah)* Under the circumstances, I have to give you a strike, Sarah. Make sure it doesn't happen again. *(To Lacy)* You may return to your grave. I can't give you a strike, but I'm quite sure that your stay here will be temporary nonetheless. To bed, everyone.

Lacy turns to Sarah, her heart bursting with gratitude. She wants to hug her, but Mrs. Steele is watching. She wants to hug Sam, too, but Mrs. Steele clears her throat, and Sarah leads the exhausted Lacy over to her small burial plot and gently encourages her to take a step in. Lacy turns and gives her a look. She can't possibly sleep. Sarah returns her gaze with a nod and the whispered advice that it is an imperative. As soon as Lacy's foot is in the grave, the rest of her descends in a quick rush. Sarah nods at Mrs. Steele and returns to her own grave. Mrs. Steele and Sam descend.

The cemetery is quiet for a moment. Far away, another siren is heard. High, high above, the tiny blinking lights of an airplane pass.

Below the stillness, the souls hum in turmoil. For decades the cemetery had settled into the dull drone of routine; sleep was so easy that it was hard to tell the difference between sleeping and rising. But now, they are unable to sleep.

[Here, dear Reader, I must pause and confess what you already know to be true: so far I have skipped rather quickly over my descriptions of the Dead in their graves. In truth, it is an image I personally don't like to linger over, given my own tendency toward claustrophobia, but I cannot do justice to the next part of this scene without giving an accurate picture. Here it is: there is nothing romantic or surprising about the graves at Westminster; they are narrow and separate and confining. So keep that in mind as you continue reading. These restless souls will be surrounded by nothing but darkness.]

Sarah, in her plain coffin, is replaying what just happened. She has turned on her side, one hand under her cheek, the other pressed against her chest. Since her grave is not far from Lacy's and since she tends to be a light sleeper, Olivia's voice had woken her. As she heard the responding emotion in Lacy's voice, her heart went out to Lacy and she found herself rising without thinking of the consequences. Inside her chest now is a mix of vibrations. She is still worried about Lacy, but she is at peace with getting her first strike, even pleased with her own boldness.

Mrs. Steele is also replaying what happened. She lies flat on her back, her hands clasped over her stomach. Sarah caught her off guard, stepping forward like that and for what reason? To save the girl? And Samuel . . . he is clearly smitten with her, too. An image of the cemetery as a quilt comes before her eyes—not a patchwork quilt, but a nicely designed pattern. She pictures the quilt stretched out, parallel to the earth, as if on a frame, and the new girl is standing on it, the weight of her threatening to pull apart the stitching that holds the pieces of fabric together. She has a fantasy that she pushes the girl off the quilt. When the girl is safely gone, she tells Effie and Neffie to reinforce the seams with tight, perfect stitches. The fantasy calms her and she falls asleep.

Lacy, unlike the others, has no coffin to define her position, and so, unlike the others, she is not lying horizontally. She is sitting, knees hugged to chest, the earth around her displaced by her soul so that she is in a kind of dark womb. Agitated beyond measure, her mind is spinning so fast she cannot feel anything but a kind of hot numbness. This is the last place she wants to be—underground, alone. But she has no choice. The cemetery feels dangerous to her, as if it has been wired with little invisible bombs that she has to, somehow, avoid detonating.

Sam is face down, hands covering his eyes, although there is nothing to see. He lies for several long minutes, flailing his mind with insults: You're being a pigeon-livered idiot. You are the king of cowards. No one with a right mind would want to spend a clock's tick of time with you. Look at Sarah! She stepped up, didn't she? She proved herself to be brave and altruistic while you shook in your boots like jelly in a jar. You might as well stay in this coffin for the rest of forever, you worthless, insubstantial sack of bones.

Sam goes on . . . he has plenty where that comes from.

Raven sits atop the monument, listening to the rat-a-tat-tat of Sam's negative vibrations, rolling his eyes.

After giving himself a thorough thrashing, Sam is spent. He turns on his side and waits for any sounds or movement from his mother's grave next to his. When she seems to be asleep, he opens his coffin and sits up, half out of his grave. He looks at Lacy's grave, not moving.

Raven flies over on silent wings and settles next to him.

Sam still does not move. With one claw, Raven withdraws the pencil from Sam's satchel and sets it in Sam's lap. Sam looks down. After a moment, he picks it up, takes out his journal, and begins to write.

Dear Lacy,

I am unable to sleep. I imagine that you are in a similar predicament, and I long to be able to offer my assistance.

Given my lack of courage earlier, you might be loath to believe me. It is our actions by which we are judged, and my actions are not worthy of admiration. I am ashamed of myself and grateful to Sarah. If you had received that third strike, it would be as if I had died again. I know we have only just met, but the initial fascination I felt for you has already grown into . . . I shall say it . . . love. I love you, Lacy Brink. Ridiculous, perhaps, but true.

Eternally yours,
Sam

Carefully Sam tears the page from his journal and rolls it. Raven reaches over with one claw and gently grasps it, making a signal with his head to show that he could play courier. But just as Raven is about to lift into the air, Sam cringes and grabs it.

SAM: I can't.

Sam stuffs the missive in his pocket. Raven tilts his head, waits to see if Sam has a change of heart.

SAM: I know. I'm a coward.

There is a long pause as an image of Sam's first love comes to him. Abigail. The oldest daughter of the lamp-lighter who lived down the street. She always had a book in her hands and was in charge of taking care of her younger siblings, walking them to school and back every day. How badly he had wanted to go to that same school, but his mother told him the school wasn't good enough. The truth, which he knew, was that his mother, being a widow, had fallen on hard times, and so Sam had to work at the sewing machine by her side in their row house, where they did piecework for a boot company. In the evening, though, Sam would often find an excuse to walk down the street where he could see the girl reading by the light of an oil lamp in her front window. Sam can almost picture it. He thinks about how he never acted on his interest in Abigail and then he looks at Lacy's unmarked grave.

SAM: She's wonderful, isn't she? Miss Lacy Brink. There's just something about her . . . *(Raven nods. Sam sighs, leans out on both elbows.)* After the last burial back in 1913, I thought my job was over and done with. I had a long stretch. Just waking up every night, writing in my journal, trying to keep from going insane. And then . . . Lacy Brink! What a surprise.

In a comic gesture, Raven wraps his wings around himself and makes the sound of kissing, but instead of laughing, Sam's face grows serious.

SAM: Please don't make fun of me tonight.

Raven bows a genuine apology, and, sensing Sam's need for privacy, turns away and settles to sleep. Sam is quiet for a long moment. Then he opens his journal. While he writes, he sings, softly at first, to Lacy's grave.

[Please, dear Reader, do not be the insensitive and hurried type who skips over poetry in favor of devouring juicy dialogue. Sam's song reveals important details. Although Lacy will not hear him, Sam is pouring out his heart to her, and you are his witness. Listen carefully.]

SAM *(singing to Lacy as he writes)*:

I know you're suffering. It's there burning in your eyes.
I want to reach out to you,
wrap you in comfort and make everything all right,
but I cannot move.

I hope you see something in me that's in you, too,
but maybe you never will.
You have experience. You have the guts I lack.
I am standing still.

I fell in love back then. Her name was Abigail.
She liked to read just like me.
There she is . . . just go and give her your poetry.
Courage is all that you need.
But I am standing still.

(Sings more forcefully now.)
I want to sing. I want to speak.
The voice inside won't let me sleep.

I want to be so different than I've been.
I spill the ink upon the page
and write my joy and write my rage
and this is what I do to ease the pain.

Sam recalls the night he came home to find his mother reading his poetry. She believed in education, but she wanted Sam to go into business. She said that poetry was a waste of time.

The war started soon after and while they worked, she often talked about how becoming a soldier could be a way for him to gain leadership skills, skills that would be useful in business. He remembers feeding the pieces of leather into the sewing machine and glancing out the window as often as possible and trying desperately to tune out her voice.

SAM *(singing)*:

How many times did I watch the trains come and go?
How many times did I dream?
I could start a new life somewhere. Make my own destiny.
Courage is all I would need.
I am standing still.

(He closes his eyes, picturing one cold, gray day.)
My mother takes me and says, "He wants to enlist.
He wants to be something more."
They give me a gun and say, "Sign your name here, boy."
Next thing I know is the war.

Marching at dawn, the ground hard underneath my boots,
head down as we climb the hill.

They're waiting for us, their muskets all loaded.
I am standing still.
Then my grave is filled.

(He looks at Lacy's grave.)
Now you have come and I feel myself waking up.
Gone is that everyday chill.
Maybe I'm here because I have to take a step
Instead of standing still.

I want to sing. I want to speak.
The voice inside won't let me sleep.
I want to be so different than I've been . . .
I spill the ink upon the page
And write my joy and write my rage—

Sam is standing now, singing his heart out with one foot in the grave when we hear a sound. Raven caws. The earthen door to Mrs. Steele's grave opens. A split second before Mrs. Steele emerges, Sam pulls his other foot into the grave.

MRS. STEELE: Samuel Steele!
SAM: Sorry, Mother. I'm not out. It was just that cat again.

Raven, behind Mrs. Steele's line of sight, puts one wing to his beak and imitates the meow. By the time Mrs. Steele turns to look, he has resumed his sleeping position.

MRS. STEELE: Enough of this nonsense and get back to bed.
SAM: Yes, Mother.

She gives the journal, which he is pressing to his chest, a disgusted look. On silent wings, Raven lifts and flies over Mrs. Steele. There is a moment of suspense and then . . . plup. An ethereal little gift lands on her head.

Sam tries to hide his smile as Mrs. Steele's face registers a wince. As she reaches up to discover the gift, Raven flies back to his perch so that he is feigning innocence by the time she looks at him. She huffs and returns to her grave.

Sam gives Raven a nod of approval.

SAM: Good night, Raven.

Raven nods. Softly, as Sam clasps his journal and descends, he sings again.

SAM *(singing)*:

And this is what I do to ease the pain
while I'm standing still.

Sam descends. His door closes. The cemetery is quiet. In the distance we hear a passing car . . . farther away a rumble of thunder . . . and then . . . silence.

SCENE 6: THE LOOPHOLE

Imperceptibly, the earth turns on its axis and is pulled along its orbit, tethered by the mysterious invisible bond of a star's love; and so our stage's set revolves inch by inch until the moon, white as a bone, has crawled to the top of the ink-black sky.

The midnight bell begins to toll. The cemetery is so still it is hard to believe anything unusual has happened within its perimeters. Then Sam's door opens with a bang. He hops out with the scroll in his hand and quickly races over to Lacy's unmarked grave. He crouches down, taps on the ground, and whispers.

SAM: Lacy, wake up! I have news.

Knowing that it will take her a moment to rouse, he runs to Sarah's grave next and does the same thing. Then he knocks softly but excitedly on Maria's grave.

By the time Maria emerges, Lacy and Sarah are out—Lacy looking exhausted and bleary-eyed—and Sam leaps into conversation without even saying hello.

SAM: There's a rule that my mother forgot—

MARIA: Goodness gracious! Your manners, Samuel.

SAM *(removing his cap)*: I'm sorry. Good evening, Mrs. Clemm. Good evening, Mrs. Brown. *(Sam's nods to Maria and Sarah are affectionate, but when he turns to greet Lacy, the full measure of his love makes his smile radiant.)* Good evening, Miss Brink.

The warmth of his greeting wakes Lacy and clears her mind. It is good to see him, she realizes. She wants to hug him—and Sarah, too, who was so sweet earlier.

SAM: I was in my grave thinking about jobs and things. I couldn't sleep. And I checked the rules and found something a few minutes ago that we all forgot. Look! *(Quickly unrolling the scroll and reading)*: "The President of the Committee to Assign Committee Assignments must interview the resident before assigning a job. Material gained from the interview should be used whenever possible to determine the most fitting job for that resident." It's Rule 219. You need to do an interview, Mrs. Clemm!

By now, Mrs. Steele and the other regulars are rising—Dr. Hosler, the Spindly sisters, Virginia, and Cumberland. They greet one another properly and then Mrs. Steele dives in.

MRS. STEELE: What's this commotion, Samuel?

Sam hides his giddiness and turns and speaks to the assembling residents in a serious, official tone.

SAM: I'm afraid we neglected to follow the rules yesterday regarding the assigning of a job for Miss Brink.

Lacy doesn't comprehend what he's talking about but she can see that Sam is excited and she gives him a smile. This sweet moment is pierced by Mrs. Steele, who marches over and gives Sam her oft-imparted swat on the back of his head.

MRS. STEELE: Samuel, are you actively trying to help this girl?

SAM: Of course not, ma'am! I thought you wanted me to study the rules.

MARIA *(stepping forward eagerly)*: I am remembering now! It's been so long since we had a new resident, I forgot. There's an interview process, Mrs. Steele, remember? And the job is supposed to be chosen based on information that is gleaned from the interview.

SAM: The interview questions are right here. *(He holds the scroll out.)* I think we should start again. There might be a more appropriate job for Miss Brink. What do you think, Mrs. Clemm? You're the President of the Committee to Assign Committee Assignments.

MARIA: I think we should start again.

Maria is about to take the scroll, but Mrs. Steele snatches it from Sam's hands and reads it.

Sam is right. It's there in black and white. Mrs. Steele straightens up and saves face by complimenting Sam even though it's obvious she is irked.

MRS. STEELE: Excellent, Samuel. How wonderful that you're keeping up. *(Turns and hands Maria the scroll.)* Mrs. Clemm, of course, we must follow the rules. Do conduct your interview.

For her part, the good-hearted Maria is much relieved.

[You should know, dear Reader, that she remembered the rule and told Mrs. Steele about it in the catacombs, but Mrs. Steele had strongly suggested that her memory was incorrect. Now Sam has spoken up, allowing her to give the poor girl a second chance.]

Hardly able to hide her happiness, Maria holds up the scroll and turns to Lacy to start the interview. Lacy sits down. The other residents lean in, and Mrs. Steele gives them all a sharp glare.

MRS. STEELE: This is official business, not a circus.

Sarah, Dr. Hosler, the Spindly sisters, Virginia, and Cumberland back up and take their usual tea places, pretending that they're not dying to hear every word. Sam climbs up onto the Watson crypt, thrilled.

Lacy sits up straight on the stone bench, knowing that she is lucky to have this opportunity, hoping that it will lead to at least some kind of improvement in her job assignment. She and Sam don't dare smile, but they exchange another look.

MARIA: Profession in life?

LACY: Um . . . I'm only sixteen.
MRS. STEELE *(interrupting with a loud huff)*: By sixteen I was married with two children and working sunup to sundown.
LACY: I'm a student. I go to school. It's kind of like a job. Was.

School seems suddenly far away to Lacy. She remembers it, but it no longer feels quite real.

MARIA: What did you study then?
LACY: I liked certain classes. I liked my English classes and chorus. Other classes seemed like a waste of time. Sometimes I'd have to pinch myself to stay awake. *(She looks at Sam and Sarah.)* I'm sure it's ridiculous for me to complain. School was probably really boring for you guys. I've seen those pictures of those wooden desks and strict teachers who hit you with rulers and made you memorize stuff. Or was school not even a thing in your time? Anyway, now it's much more informal. I'm sure it's much noisier. I like the library. Mrs. O'Reilly let me come in during lunch. And Mr. Vincent, the music teacher, is a really good teacher. I actually learn stuff in his class. And every day you see all the people you like. *(She looks at Sam.)* Everybody acts . . . there's just more . . . openness. We hug a lot. Every day when you see your friends—I don't know—you hug. It's nice. You can kind of be who you are. I mean, that's not completely true. You think everything's great and then something will happen, like a hate crime. And you realize there are still haters out there.

Sam loves the sound of her voice. He'd like to sit there and listen to her talk all night. He wants to know everything about her. He wants to know what that library is like. He wants to know what it's like to be hugged every day.

MRS. STEELE: Let's get to the point.
MARIA: Family?
LACY: My dad abandoned us. Not in a drug addict, criminal kind of way, more like in a workaholic way. He's a lawyer and was never home, and then when I was ten his firm wanted to send him to Dubai to set up a big international office there and my mom said forget it and he said well I'm going. My mom is a high school math teacher, which is funny because I'm not the math type. Or the lawyer type. Neither is Liv, my sister, come to think of it. My mom teaches at a school in Towson—not the one we go to. She's a worrier, my mom. She's always calling me and texting me and getting freaked out if I don't text back.

Lacy looks out at the street beyond the iron gate, realizing that she keeps talking in the present tense. That ache in her throat returns.

LACY: I used to think my mom was overreacting and that she didn't need to worry so much, but bad things do happen . . . It's really hard for me to imagine . . . This whole thing must be so hard for her . . . I wonder how she found out. Did the police knock on the door? Do they know who did this to me? Is the guy in jail? She must be so angry and sad—

The residents are quiet. Mrs. Steele shifts uncomfortably in her seat and clears her throat for Maria to continue.

MARIA: Any other family?

LACY: My sister, Olivia. *(Looks up at Maria.)* She was here earlier, at the cemetery. I think she came to visit me. I wanted to ask her what happened to me . . . I know that sounds ridiculous. I know she can't hear me. *(She looks at Sam, who gives her a sympathetic nod.)* Anyway, she's eighteen. We're different. I love books and words and music *(Sam's soul is swooning)* and she's all about partying and hanging with this huge group of friends. She does a lot of stuff that my mom would freak out about but she's really good at lying. *(Lacy's face darkens.)*

Sam wants to respond, but his mother interrupts with a huff.

MRS. STEELE *(to Maria)*: How many questions are there, Mrs. Clemm?

MARIA: Just two more.

Sam is disappointed. Would that there were ten more, twenty more, a thousand more.

MARIA: Do you have any habits that might be relevant to a particular job?

LACY: Habits? I don't know—

MRS. STEELE *(peering at Lacy's hands)*: She bites her nails.

Reflexively Lacy pulls her hands in. Will Mrs. Steele try to argue that this makes her perfectly suited to eating termites? A tremor of anxiety runs through Lacy. She hasn't been focusing. She has to think of something that will help her get a better job, but how can she when she is at such a disadvantage? She doesn't even know the range of possibilities.

MARIA: Last question. Were you particularly suited for any recreational diversions, such as fern-collecting or hat-making?

LACY: Hobbies? *(Pause. She tries to consider what might be useful to say, but in the end can only think of the truth.)* Spoken word. I sing and I rap—

Raven perks up at the word *rap* and caws abruptly.

MARIA: Rap on doors?

LACY: Rap . . . like lyrics . . . poetry.

VIRGINIA *(rolling her eyes)*: More poetry.

Thrilled, Sam moves to the edge of the crypt. An affirming hum is vibrating out from him, and Lacy can feel the energy.

MARIA: Poetry?

Maria's energy is humming, too. And Sarah's. Lacy can feel it all. She has kindred spirits here, and that fans her own flames. She stands. An idea is coming to her.

LACY: I know what I should do.

Everyone is silent, unused to hearing such assertiveness, especially coming from someone as young as Lacy.

The residents, with the exception of Mrs. Steele, lean in, eager to hear what this girl has to say.

MRS. STEELE: It is not the resident who chooses his or her job.

SAM: There's nothing in the rules to say that a resident can't give a suggestion.

Mrs. Steele gives Sam a sharp look, but he pretends not to see it.

MARIA: What did you have in mind, Miss Brink?

LACY *(with even more conviction)*: I want to run an open mic.

MRS. STEELE: What in the world is that?

LACY: It's short for open microphone. *(She paces, her face flushing, her eyes shining.)* How can I explain this? A microphone is a round, knobby thing that projects your voice so an audience can hear it. An open mic is entertainment . . . but it's not formal or scripted. It's kind of like a show, but it doesn't happen in a theater. It usually happens at a . . . well, at a place that serves tea and coffee or beer and wine.

SARAH *(excited)*: We serve tea.

Mrs. Steele shoots her a look and Sarah quickly wipes the excitement off her face.

SARAH: Sorry, ma'am. I heard the word "tea."

EFFIE *(to Lacy)*: Entertainment . . . what do you mean?

LACY: People get up and perform their poems or their songs.

Sam hops off the Watson crypt. He can't believe his good fortune.

MRS. STEELE: People? What do you mean by "people"?

LACY: Anybody who wants to. Somebody is the emcee and you have a sign-up sheet and anybody can come and sign up to perform.

SAM: Anybody?

LACY *(smiles)*: Anybody. The whole idea is to create a space for self-expression, to give people a chance to share their poems or their music with a supportive crowd. I mean, the vibe at most open mics is very—I don't know how to explain it. It's just very real and raw. Sometimes the performers aren't great, but everybody is rooting for them because they're letting it out, they're taking the risk, putting their heart and soul into it. Most people do original poems or songs, things they have written or something that expresses the truth of what they're feeling. Do you know what I mean?

Silence. Collectively, the souls gathered in front of Lacy have spent hundreds of days, weeks, months, years hiding various truths from each other and from themselves. To stand up in front of others and to, as she says, "let it out" seems impossible. They glance at each other, each trying to imagine the unimaginable.

Sam steps into the privacy of a shadow and pulls out his journal to see if there is anything inside that he might have the courage to share. Sarah looks down at her shoes, thoughts racing. Effie reaches over and squeezes Neffie's hand. Maria glances at Dr. Hosler, who raises his eyebrows with a smile as if to say, "Well, this is unexpected, isn't it?" Finally Mrs. Steele breaks the silence.

MRS. STEELE: I've never heard of such a thing. One should keep one's thoughts and emotions to one's self.

MARIA: Agreed, of course, Mrs. Steele. But it would be nice to have some kind of entertainment.

Lacy nods, hoping others will speak up in favor of the idea.

DR. HOSLER: Once, when I was teaching a class of medical students, a young man brought in a sonnet that he had written about caring for his sick grandmother. It wasn't academic. It was personal. When he read it aloud, I was brought to tears.

LACY: That's what I mean! It can be really beautiful.

SARAH: It would take great courage to share something so personal.

NEFFIE *(encouraged to be a little bolder)*: I think this open mic idea sounds educational as well as entertaining.

EFFIE: If we allowed her to do it, we would be creating a new job . . . do our bylaws allow us to create new jobs?

MARIA *(quickly before Mrs. Steele can respond)*: It wouldn't be a new job. She would be President of the Entertainment Committee. We used to have one, remember?

DR. HOSLER: Clarissa Smythe, if I recall. She organized evenings of parlor songs and dances that were quite entertaining!

From Clarissa's grave, her voice calls out.

CLARISSA: Thank you, Dr. Hosler!

Owen looks up. With the exception of Mrs. Steele, there are smiles all around as the residents recall the brief sweet period of nightly tunes and dances. Miffed at Clarissa for speaking out, Mrs. Steele readies herself to summon Owen if she tries it again. But Clarissa is silent.

MRS. STEELE: Entertainment is risky. Let us recall that on the third night of performances, Miss Smythe got quite carried away. That song with the innuendos earned her a third strike.

[At the mention of this, you will notice, if you are observant, that Owen looks as if he has been struck in the chest with an arrow.

A further glance at the expressions of the others will tell you what you probably have already guessed, dear Reader: that no one but Mrs. Steele thought the song "with the innuendos" was worthy of a strike.]

NEFFIE: I remember.
EFFIE: That was the last show. Nobody came along that was suited to fill the position after that.

A sad silence follows. Finally Maria throws in one last seemingly fruitless appeal.

MARIA: Perhaps with our help Miss Brink can ensure that the material will be appropriate.

Mrs. Steele is quiet. All are expecting her to reject the idea, but Mrs. Steele smiles.

MRS. STEELE: Fine.

Raven does a double take. Everyone is shocked.

MARIA: Fine?

MRS. STEELE: Perfect.

VIRGINIA: Perfect?

MRS. STEELE *(to Lacy)*: You will organize and host an open mic. And we hope you will also perform.

LACY: I—I haven't really thought about that.

MRS. STEELE *(smiling thinly)*: You must. We're dying to see what you do. Why don't you get started? I imagine you have to prepare a few things before showtime.

LACY: Now?

MRS. STEELE: No time like the present.

Mrs. Steele folds her hands in her lap and smiles, looking like a villain who has just poured a cup of poison and is waiting for her nemesis to take a sip.

SCENE 7: THE TRANSFORMATION

Despite Mrs. Steele's attitude, something positive is happening. As Lacy looks at Sam and the other assembled residents, she can feel it. She hears a new hum, a faint buzzing sound that is growing in intensity. Although it sounds alive, it isn't frightening. It sounds, to Lacy, like the tremolo of bows against strings, but it is, in fact, the hum that the souls of the Deceased give off when some extraordinary current of new energy is beginning to run through old grounds.

Lacy nods and smiles.

LACY: Okay. Let's do this.

The Spindly sisters jump to their feet like schoolgirls and start plotting.

EFFIE: We should have a little stage, perhaps something exotic . . . columns on the side with Rosicrucian symbols?
NEFFIE: Oooh, some velvet draperies!
EFFIE: And on each table . . . nosegays!
NEFFIE: Decorative placecards!
EFFIE: Come, Virginia, you're the President of the Decorating Committee! This will be fun.

NEFFIE: Doilies!
EFFIE: Nut cups are always a nice touch.

Although Virginia is dying for entertainment, her jealousy of Lacy keeps her firmly planted in her seat. She has no desire to help make more of a celebrity out of the girl. In fact, she thinks throwing a little water on Lacy's fire might be fun.

VIRGINIA: Ladies . . . calm down. It's not as if there's a mercantile down the street.
EFFIE: Right. We'll make use of what we have.

Cumberland, who has been playing it safe by sitting near his crypt and keeping his mouth closed, can no longer contain his excitement.

CUMBERLAND *(standing up)*: I happen to have a silk sheet in my crypt! My mother wanted me tucked in, so to speak. Perhaps we could get the effect of a small stage by hanging the sheet up between two posts of the iron gate. Look! *(He points to an open space between the Watson and Hosler crypts.)* With my sheet hung up like a curtain in the back, it would define the space as a stage, don't you think?

Virginia gives Cumberland a dirty look, but the sisters clap and coo and Maria joins the excited huddle.

MARIA: It will be nice to have something more than tea to look forward to. *(She gives a quick apologetic glance to Sarah.)* No offense, Sarah. You make a lovely pot of tea.

SARAH: No offense taken, Mrs. Clemm.

EFFIE: Ladies! We could spread our shawls on the sarcophagi . . . here, in front of the open space, and they could serve as the tables!

NEFFIE: The tombstones behind them and around them could be our chairs.

Dr. Hosler rises, too. He recalls that bubbling of excitement one feels in the chest when a theatrical spectacle begins, and he wouldn't mind feeling it again.

DR. HOSLER: Happy to help out in whatever way I can. Perhaps the host would like to borrow my hat?

With a grin, he tosses his top hat at Lacy. She catches it, puts it on, and smiles adorably, first at the doctor and then at Sam, whose heart skips several beats.

Mrs. Steele's eyes flash, but she remains quiet.

Lacy can feel Mrs. Steele's hostility, and lace shawls and silk sheets aren't exactly the hip vibe she had in mind, but the warm enthusiasm from the group is seeping into Lacy and filling her with the desire to make this work, to give them a positive experience. She faces them.

LACY: Creating the effect of a stage and tables would be great. *(She smiles at Sarah.)* If we could have tea along with the entertainment, that would be perfect.

SARAH *(beams)*: I can do that!

Sarah jumps up and begins preparations for tea, and the excited residents transform the crumbling graveyard

into a little café of sorts as Lacy paces, rehearsing what she'll say to kick off the show. The Spindly sisters set their lace shawls like tablecloths upon three sarcophagi and collect small bouquets from the residents who were buried with them to use as centerpieces.

Much to Virginia's annoyance, Cumberland leaps into action with more verve than she has ever seen from him, hanging up his silk sheet from the iron gate between the two sets of crypts.

Delighted to have a project, Dr. Hosler uses his scalpel to cut letters spelling *Open Mic Night at Westminster Cemetery* out of the pillowcase from his own coffin. As soon as he is done, he hangs this up like a poster on the iron gate near the backdrop curtain. The moonlight shining through the negative spaces of the pillowcase makes it look as if the letters are lit up.

Meanwhile, Sam is feverishly revising a poem, looking every now and then at Lacy with starry eyes to make sure her appearance in this place isn't a dream.

DR. HOSLER: What do you think, Miss Brink?

Lacy takes it all in.

LACY: Sweet. And oddly charming.
EFFIE: The place has never looked better.
NEFFIE: All we need is an audience.

Reality hits Lacy like a bolt of lightning. It's one thing to decorate, but can she count on anyone here to actually come through with a performance?

LACY: Um . . . the audience is the easy part. Are any of you going to perform?

Sam catches her eye and a terrified look comes over his face. The poem in his hands suddenly seems awkward and inelegant. If he shared it and it didn't go well, Lacy's admiration for him would plummet. He walks over to the urn where he stuffs his rejects and squashes it in.

Lacy sees it happening before her eyes. Stage fright and a lack of confidence make for a terrible combination. If Sam won't perform, she wonders, who will? She looks around. Sarah is too timid. The Spindly sisters and Maria are more the type to cheer rather than to perform. Virginia definitely has something to say, and Lacy is guessing that she would have a ton of stage presence; but when Lacy looks over at her, she sees the smirk Virginia is giving her and feels even further disheartened. Virginia wants her to fail. Mean girls always do.

Perched on Poe's monument, Raven clears his throat loudly. Lacy looks at the bird. He clears his throat again and then looks down, as if to call attention to the base of the monument. The letters P-O-E come into focus.

LACY: Edgar Allan Poe! I can't believe I forgot about him. I'm having an open mic in Edgar Allan Poe's cemetery! *(She looks at the monument and then back at Raven.)* Oh my Go— sh. You're the Raven! He wrote a famous poem about you.

Raven gives a dignified nod. Everything Lacy learned for her seventh-grade report on Poe and his family rushes back. She spins around and looks at Virginia.

LACY: You're his wife! I can't believe I'm just making this connection. You're Virginia Clemm Poe.

Virginia gives a complicated, rueful smile, a smile that totally intrigues Lacy, a smile that Lacy wants to unpack when she has the time, which she doesn't at the moment; and then Maria clears her throat, and Lacy spins around to face her.

LACY: And you're his aunt and mother-in-law, Maria Clemm. I recognized you when we first met, but with all the drama, the whole Poe connection slipped my mind. He used to call you Muddy. You ran the house. You were very well organized.

MARIA *(pleased)*: Thank you. I've missed Eddy.

Virginia rolls her eyes and then she notices everyone—including Mrs. Steele—looking at her and adds a quick amendment.

VIRGINIA: Of course I miss my husband, too. Any wife would. *(To gain favor with Mrs. Steele she adds)* But Eddy has no one to blame but himself. Anyone who gets three strikes has to live with the consequences.

LACY *(shocked)*: What?

SAM: Mr. Poe is Suppressed.

LACY: No fu—dging way.

SAM: We never really got to know him. From what I heard, it took him a long time to rise for the first time.

EFFIE: Weeks.

VIRGINIA *(under her breath)*: Probably had to sleep off the drink.

EFFIE: When he finally rose, it was three strikes in the first three minutes.

NEFFIE: Poor Mr. Poe.

MRS. STEELE: He didn't have to be so verbal in his dislike for the rules. If he hadn't been, he wouldn't have gotten his strikes.

MARIA: Well, he has been silent ever since.

VIRGINIA *(under her breath again)*: Probably *still* sleeping off the drink.

MARIA: Virginia!

VIRGINIA *(shrugs and whispers)*: He drank a lot.

LACY: He got strikes for expressing his dislike of the rules? That isn't right.

MRS. STEELE: He received strikes for throwing a tantrum.

LACY: I can't believe that you've essentially silenced one of America's famous poets.

MRS. STEELE: We didn't silence him. He silenced himself by behaving inappropriately.

There is a beat of silence. Lacy can feel that the majority of the residents disagree with the system, but they remain quiet.

EFFIE: Well, since we can't have Mr. Poe, perhaps a poet will come out of the woodwork, so to speak. Someone who has been writing poetry secretly could surprise us with a masterpiece.

Sam reaches back into the urn and sifts through the discarded pages, hoping against hope to find a gem, an action that Mrs. Steele notices with disdain.

MARIA: Why don't we ask Peter to make an announcement around the entire perimeter? Who knows, perhaps some of our younger residents will be interested in participating. *(Everyone looks at Mrs. Steele to see what she thinks, and Maria jumps in.)* After all, it would be rude to have a soiree and not inform those with aboveground privileges.

Maria has a point, and Mrs. Steele is obliged to nod. Delighted, Maria marches over to Peter Brown's grave and knocks. Peter steps out, surprised.

MARIA: Peter, we have a job for you! We want you to announce our new entertainment. Let's call it a talent show so people understand. Say: "Poetry talent show starting soon." Make sure to do it around the entire cemetery. Say: "All who have aboveground privileges are welcome."

Mrs. Steele nods at the shocked Peter to get on with it. Then she takes a seat toward the rear of the cemetery, in the shadows, so that she can collect her thoughts. She is allowing the open mic because she thinks it will provide an opportunity for the girl to break a rule. She only hopes that the mounting enthusiasm doesn't have any ill effects for Westminster on the whole.

Excited, Peter pulls his bell out and begins to make the rounds.

PETER: Oyez! Oyez! Come one, come all who have aboveground privileges! Poetry talent show starting soon! All are welcome! Oyez! Oyez!

He begins to walk around the cemetery, repeating his call.

EFFIE: I wonder if the announcement will do any good.

MARIA: It might encourage some to wake up and step out for a change. We might see old friends. If so, it will be quite the affair! Quite the how-de-do!

VIRGINIA *(barely able to contain her sarcasm)*: Oh yes. Quite the how-de-do.

NEFFIE: Perhaps Mr. Barr will rise. *(She turns to Lacy.)* He plays a lovely tin whistle.

VIRGINIA: He's been sleeping since 1899. I doubt this will inspire him to join us.

DR. HOSLER: You could perform, Virginia.

VIRGINIA: I am not performing in Miss Brink's little talent show.

As Virginia is speaking, William "Billy" Bodley appears from the back of the cemetery, buttoning up the jacket of his Civil War uniform and putting on his cap.

A sixteen-year-old drummer for the Baltimore regiment, he was buried with his drumsticks in the same section of the cemetery as Owen, a collection of much more modest graves.

Sam, who was just about to stuff the poem he is holding back into the urn, looks up along with the others and shrinks.

[Perhaps, dear Reader, I need to explain that Sam is not literally becoming smaller. Since you do not know all the rules of the afterlife, you might assume that shrinking is a possibility. I am using the word here to describe that deflating of self-esteem

that can come when one rather sensitive soul has to watch a much more confident soul enter the scene. If you have never had to face that little demon called jealousy, you are lucky. Unfortunately, Billy Bodley's arrival is a challenge for Sam and you're going to have to watch poor Sam squirm. I'll explain why soon. For now, please keep him in your thoughts.]

BILLY: Did I hear something about entertainment?

Virginia turns.

With a dazzling grin, the precociously charming Billy tips his cap to all the ladies. His hair is long, and he runs his hand through it to keep a few locks from falling into his eyes, a habit that could be annoying but, coupled with a dimpled smile, makes him irresistible.

Seeing that he has an audience, he tosses his cap onto the head of a stone angel, pulls his drumsticks out of his back pocket, and twirls them around.

The eyes of all the women—with the exception of Mrs. Steele—and at least one of the men light up.

EFFIE *(whispering to Neffie)*: It's Billy. Remember Billy?
NEFFIE *(whispering back)*: I remember when he got his first strike!

Shortly after Billy Bodley's Official Welcome on a hot summer night, he made the mistake of ditching his jacket and his undershirt, which was purely for effect, thus exposing his young and muscular chest and arms—a sight that many in the graveyard greatly enjoyed, but for which he was given his first strike.

VIRGINIA *(stepping forward with as much of a flirtatious smile as can be allowed under Mrs. Steele's gaze)*: Why, Billy Bodley, we haven't seen you in ages.

BILLY: Ginny Poe. A sight for sore eyes. Hello, gals. *(He winks at the Spindly sisters and they giggle.)* Gents.

Virginia beams and extends her hand, expecting Billy to kiss it the way he did when he first woke up at Westminster. Instead he strides past her and takes Lacy's hand in his. Sam watches Lacy, whose jaw has dropped slightly.

BILLY: Who's this filly? And why've I been asleep so long?

Under Billy's intense gaze, Lacy squirms. But not without pleasure, Sam notices.

Virginia is seething.

LACY: Hi.

BILLY: Name's Billy. I love your hat.

LACY *(blushing and taking off Dr. Hosler's top hat)*: Oh. Thank you.

MARIA: Wonderful to see you again, Mr. Bodley!

DR. HOSLER *(clapping Billy on the back)*: Bacterial infection following a wound, if I recall.

MARIA *(to Lacy)*: Billy was a drummer in the war, and that was a serious responsibility. They communicated messages and commands by relaying different rhythms. Quite a talent.

EFFIE: And so brave! When his best friend, a soldier, was shot, Billy ran to carry him back to safety. He was shot in the back.

NEFFIE: Poor brave lamb.

Everyone looks at Billy. Sam winces.

From her seat in the rear of the cemetery, Mrs. Steele is about to put an end to this ridiculous tongue-waggling. She never liked Billy Bodley. Too much of a show-off. But then, she thinks, the boy could be just the thing to push Lacy Brink over the edge of propriety. She folds her hands and presses her lips together.

Lacy sees the first true potential for a performer in Billy and she doesn't hesitate.

LACY: We're having what's called an "open mic." It's like a talent show.

EFFIE: Perhaps you could add your talents, Billy.

NEFFIE: Miss Lacy Brink here is the host.

EFFIE: She's a Modern.

BILLY *(smiling broadly at Lacy)*: I can tell! How can I help, Miss Lacy Brink? Need a drummer?

Billy goes down on one knee and taps out a light rhythm on the toes of Lacy's boots with his drumsticks. She laughs and looks down at him. The thought of having someone else around who is young and energetic and musical lifts her spirits.

VIRGINIA: I'd love to watch you perform, Billy! I'm considering performing myself.

Lacy laughs at Virginia's sudden desire to perform in the show she had derided only minutes ago, and Virginia gives her a look.

LACY: Actually, Billy, it would be great to have a drummer. A lot of spoken word is rhythm-based.
BILLY: Spoken word?
LACY: You lay down a beat and then the poet raps over you.
BILLY *(with a twinkling smile)*: You can rap over me any time—

The sight of Billy on one knee gazing up at Lacy with his hair falling into his eyes and the sight of Lacy looking back at him with a smile on her face sends Sam into full-blown panic. He has to do something—the only problem is that he doesn't know what.

BILLY *(stands)*: I'm willing and able.
LACY: We aren't quite ready yet. We still need a sign-up sheet—a paper where people who want to perform can write their names.

Raven gives Sam an encouraging caw and a look that says, "Lacy needs a sign-up sheet, man, so snap to it."

Sam leaps forward, opening his satchel to offer his help, when Billy sees Sam's journal and pencil and grabs them both with an affable smile.

BILLY: Thanks!

Billy writes "Sign up here to preform!" in Sam's journal, rips the page out, and hands it to Lacy along with the pencil.

[Yes, dear Reader, I am as outraged as you are. To grab anything out of anyone's satchel is plain rude. Even if Billy is

being cluelessly enthusiastic, the moment should belong to Sam. But look! Lacy's soul is just as sensitive as ours and she's about to fix things.]

LACY *(smiling at them both)*: Thank you, Billy. But Sam should keep track of the sign-up sheet since it's his pencil and paper. Will you hold onto these, Sam? Whoever wants to sign up will need to borrow your pencil.

SAM *(taking the items from her with a relieved smile)*: Yes, of course! I'd be delighted.

BILLY *(feeling the first prick of jealousy)*: I'll be too busy drumming anyway. On stage. With Miss Lacy.

SAM *(after a glance at the writing on the sheet)*: Yes, well, from the way you've misspelled the word *perform*, I'd say that a drumstick is a better instrument for you than a pencil, Billy.

[Ha! Good one, Sam—you might be saying—that's the way to let him have it! It is amusing to see rivals jabbing at each other, isn't it, dear Reader? There is, however, an important key difference between Sam and Billy that you should know. Unlike Billy, who stalks off because he can't think of a witty retort, a wince of regret crosses Sam's face as soon as he lets the quip fly. The Golden Rule—the one that says you should treat people as you would like to be treated—has always been the one rule that has made perfect sense to Sam, and he knows that his impulsive jab at Billy just now was immature. Lacy, who can't help feeling pleased that these two are both trying to win points with her, sees Sam wince and thinks it is adorable. Unfortunately, she doesn't say so outright and Sam is too busy looking down to see her smile, and so he will miss this confidence stimulator.]

Suddenly, the voices of the Spindly sisters capture everyone's attention.

EFFIE: Mrs. Babbitt!
NEFFIE: Mr. Babbitt!

Peter's announcement has roused a dozen Sleepers out of the graves, residents with one or two strikes whose curiosity has pushed them to rise. For the regulars, it is a reunion of old friends. Effie and Neffie rush to greet Mildred and George Babbitt, a couple with whom they used to enjoy playing a card game called Whist. Explanations about the evening are given and several brave souls cluster around Sam to sign up. As the preparations and salutations continue and Sarah happily rushes to serve tea, no one seems to notice the usually pervasive Mrs. Steele, who is sitting still with her face toward the stage, trying very hard to hold onto the belief that this entire affair will not get out of hand.

MARIA: I think everything is ready, Miss Brink. We should begin the show.

Lacy looks out. The residents are perched on tombstones in front of and around the space designated as the "stage." The regulars—the Spindly sisters, Maria, Dr. Hosler—are sitting with the newcomers, chatting and already having a nice time. Sarah is standing in the rear with her teapot, ready to refill teacups as needed. Billy is on one side, waiting to help. Sam is on the other, holding the sign-up sheet. Virginia has taken a seat a few feet from all the others. Cumberland, not knowing where to sit, stands awkwardly by the doorway of his crypt.

Nervous but excited, Lacy steps forward to begin and then realizes what's missing.

LACY: The microphone!

The regulars look at each other. Of course no one has been buried with a microphone. None of them has ever seen one. Lacy's distress touches Sam and he steps forward, but Billy beats him to Lacy's side.

BILLY *(whispers to Lacy)*: What does it look like?

Lacy whispers a quick description in his ear. Billy's eyes light up, and he runs over to George Babbitt and borrows his cane. With a bold flourish, he shoves the cane into the ground in front of Lacy, pulls a kerchief out of his pocket, and polishes the lovely silver knob at the top. Voilà. A "microphone" of sorts, at just the right height for Lacy.

LACY: Thank you.
BILLY *(beams)*: Your happiness is mine.

Sam clenches his fists in frustration, and then, realizing that he has just crumpled the sign-up sheet, catches himself and smooths it out. He is determined to find the next opportunity to impress Lacy. Perhaps, if he can find the courage, he will even perform a poem!

SCENE 8: SHOWTIME

With the moon hanging like a spotlight in the black sky, Lacy steps up to the microphone, top hat on. Billy is on her left. Sam is on her right. To her delight, the crowd keeps chatting, so thrilled to be out, so happy to be participating in some form of communal entertainment that they don't even notice that she's ready to begin. Even Owen Hapliss is responding. Although he is still at his spot against the side wall of the church, he has turned to face the stage, and his back is straight, his eyes bright. Lacy smiles and waves at him to come forward, to take a seat closer. Shock sweeps over his face, and he shakes his head. This girl is sweet but naïve, he thinks. No one here would want him to sit near them.

Billy taps his drumsticks against a tombstone to get the audience's attention.

LACY: Hi . . . Welcome to Open Mic Night at Westminster Cemetery. *(Quite suddenly the crowd hushes, and Lacy's legs begin to shake.)* Wow. It's so quiet. Um . . . Um . . .

Sam knows a thing or two about nervousness, and he can tell that Lacy's mind has gone blank. He waves the sign-up sheet at her and his sweet, helpful expression gives her the boost she needs.

LACY: Okay. Before the show begins, let me explain how it works. Sam has the sign-up sheet. *(She smiles.)* Thank you, Sam. At any time during the show, you can add your name to the list if you want to perform. I'll start at the top of the list. When I call your name, just come up. Let's be supportive and make it an atmosphere that feels safe and open. Everybody's welcome.

Without a word of warning, Mrs. Steele steps out of the shadows and walks toward the stage. At the sight of her, George and Mildred Babbitt get up quietly and return to their graves. Billy quickly reclaims his cap from the stone angel statue on which he had so casually thrown it and hastily buttons up his jacket.

With a cold smile, Mrs. Steele chooses to perch on a tombstone near the open area that is serving as the stage, a spot where everyone can see her. She turns and catches Sarah's attention to bring her a cup of tea.

Six more residents get up and return quickly to their graves, Cumberland Poltroon among them. Virginia rolls her eyes at his cowardice. Just when things are getting interesting, she thinks to herself.

Lacy knows what the old woman is doing. It's brilliant. She's using her own presence like a weapon, reminding everybody that she'll be watching for the slightest act of impropriety. She might as well have stood up and read a warning. Those who are remaining in their seats look terrified. Some of them probably want to go to their graves, too, but are afraid to even do that.

Sarah comes around behind Mrs. Steele with the tea, her hand shaking so much the cup is rattling against the saucer. As she passes by Raven, perched on Poe's monument, the bird quickly turns, lifts his tail, and adds a tidy dollop of seasoning to the tea. Everyone but Mrs. Steele sees this. A stunned Sarah stands frozen, looking into the teacup.

Mrs. Steele notices Sarah, beckons her over, grabs the teacup from her, and takes a sip. Quickly Sarah returns to her post.

Smiles are hidden.

Virginia, who wouldn't dare tattle on Raven, does see an opportunity to gain points with Mrs. Steele. She moves to Mrs. Steele's table and asks if she can join her, and Mrs. Steele motions for her to sit down.

The two women clink their teacups and then look at Lacy with almost identical smirks.

It's enough to make Lacy scream, which is exactly what Mrs. Steele wants. Lacy feels the anger rising and struggles to keep it under control.

Sam wants to help, but he can't think of anything to do.

After another moment or two of silence, Mrs. Steele speaks.

MRS. STEELE *(loudly)*: If this is what the Moderns call a performance, I must say I'm confused.

Virginia laughs and a few of those who feel a need to ingratiate themselves with Mrs. Steele follow suit.

Lacy wants so badly to call them both out, to say that they are being bitches and everybody knows it.

Mrs. Steele can see it in her eyes and leans forward eagerly.

Lacy will not give up. She takes the sign-up sheet from Sam and returns to the mic.

LACY *(defiantly)*: We are going to have a great show. See, this is what I'm talking about. *(She holds up the sheet.)* Seven people who I don't even know have signed up. That's amazing. That's seven people who have something inside of them that they want to share, and here is the opportunity they've been waiting for. Give it up for . . . Rosalind Boyd. *(The audience is silent. Lacy realizes they don't know what "give it up" means.)* Let's have some applause. Come on up, Rosalind!

The audience applauds. No one comes forward. The applause dies out and there is an awkward silence.

VIRGINIA *(happy to deliver the bad news)*: I believe she went back to sleep.

Mrs. Steele chortles. Lacy gives her a look.

LACY: No problem. *(Reading the next name on the sign-up sheet)* Okay, let's welcome Edmund Harris. *(Another round of applause. No one steps forward. Lacy moves to the next name.)* Edith Robb?

A girl sitting at a table on the side quickly gets up, and Lacy begins to breathe a sigh of relief, but then she runs toward the back and dives into her grave.

LACY *(to Mrs. Steele)*: You're scaring them away.
MRS. STEELE: Me? I'm just sitting here enjoying my tea. *(She takes another sip.)* A little salty tonight, Sarah.

Raven coughs.

Lacy reads the other names on the sheet and no one steps forward.

Sam wants to rescue Lacy, but the only thing that would really help her now would be to stand up and perform. Raven nods at him as if to say, "You can do it!" Sam is about to step forward, and a grateful Lacy sees this, when Virginia calls out.

VIRGINIA: Why don't you show us how it's done, Miss Brink?
MRS. STEELE: Wonderful idea, Virginia. Please do, Miss Brink. Recite us one of your poems. You promised us entertainment.
BILLY: I'll help! I'll give you that beat you were talking about.

Before either Lacy or Sam can object, Billy beats out a rhythm with his sticks and the audience happily claps along.

MRS. STEELE *(straightening up with mock interest)*: Ah, we're finally going to hear a poem.

Lacy wants desperately to rise above the negative vibes and deliver a piece, something that will prove to Mrs. Steele and to everyone here that people like Mrs. Steele can't win. She closes her eyes and listens to the rhythm, but she keeps seeing the mean old woman's imposing glare in her mind's eye.

MRS. STEELE: Am I missing something? I thought a poem had words.

Lacy feels something inside her deflate in a rush. She steps back from the mic, and the rhythm dies out. Mrs. Steele leans forward, hoping Lacy will explode. Instead Lacy turns her back to the audience, furious and humiliated. Sam tries to think of something to say to Lacy, but Billy simply drops his sticks and rushes to her side.

Mrs. Steele stands.

MRS. STEELE: The show is over, ladies and gentlemen. Clearly Miss Brink misled us. She can't provide us with entertainment of even the most basic kind. According to Rule 246, any resident who appears to be unsuitable to a given assignment can be given a different assignment. Mrs. Clemm, I suggest that, regardless of her interview, this girl did a better job at collecting termites than hosting an open mic and so she should resume her position on the Termite Collection Committee.

With a pop, Mrs. Steele removes the cane "microphone" from the ground. She marches over to George Babbitt's grave and knocks. When his arm emerges from the grave, she shoves the cane into his hand, and the arm and cane descend out of sight. Next she marches back to the stage, lifts Dr. Hosler's top hat off Lacy's head and, with a surprisingly athletic snap, sends it sailing directly back to its owner. Finally, she turns to Lacy and smiles, waiting for her reaction. Determined not to crack, Lacy doesn't move.

MRS. STEELE *(turning to the remaining crowd)*: Even though it is early, I suggest that everyone get to bed. We've already had our tea.

It is taking longer than Mrs. Steele thought for Lacy to get her third strike. She hoped the mere appearance of Billy would bring out the girl's indiscretion. Then she was sure that Lacy's disappointment over the open mic would do it. Well, it isn't over yet, she thinks. Without another word, she retires to her grave and closes the door behind her.

Most of the other residents hurry off to their graves; it is painful for them to watch the young newcomer suffer and to be powerless to help.

Now, it's just Raven perched, as usual, on Poe's monument; Owen in the shadows against the wall; Billy and Lacy on the stage; and Sam off to the side. Hesitantly, Sam walks up to them, trying to find a way to interrupt. Their backs are to him. As Sam approaches, he can hear what Billy is saying.

BILLY: You have every right to be mad, Miss Lacy.

LACY: It's just not fair for one person to have so much power over everybody.

BILLY: Well, it's over now. Why don't you come along and sit with me? There's a nice view from my gravestone. Your troubles will seem smaller from there. *(With a dimpled smile)* I guarantee it.

Sam can't bear it. Mistakenly, he thinks he can't compete with Billy. He turns and runs to his grave, telling himself that he has lost her. If Lacy goes into Billy's grave and they get caught, that's the end of her. If Lacy goes into Billy's grave and they don't get caught, they'll probably fall in love. Either way, Sam is out. At his grave, he turns and gives her one last look, and then he leaps inside.

In the next second, Lacy pulls away from Billy, turns to see an empty graveyard, and her heart breaks. She was hoping to see Sam. He must be too afraid of getting in trouble to think of hanging out with her. Still, she didn't think he would go to bed without even saying good night.

BILLY: What do you say, Miss Lacy?

As Lacy turns back to face Billy, the door to Mrs. Steele's grave opens a crack. The old woman peeks out, ready to pounce.

LACY: Thanks for the offer. But I think I need to be alone.

Mrs. Steele scowls.

BILLY: My coffin is small, of course, but . . . *(whispering with a smile)* we could get away from all these stiff collars.
LACY: Thanks, Billy, but I've got to think things through alone.
BILLY *(points)*: I'm right over there if you need me.
LACY: See you tomorrow.

Lacy turns and Mrs. Steele quickly ducks back down. Billy retrieves his drumsticks and saunters back to his grave.

Lacy sits on her bench, and over the next few minutes, Mrs. Steele peeks out. When she sees that Lacy is unlikely to get into trouble by herself, she gives up and goes to sleep.

One by one the residents fall asleep in their graves, and the energy of the graveyard changes. The silence is deeper.

Clouds drift in front of the moon, and Raven looks up. Lacy looks up, too. At the sight of the familiar white orb, both the girl and the bird fall into meditation.

[You, dear Reader, surely have had this experience. After a whirlwind of a day, you find yourself, quite by accident, noticing the moon, and something about its gentle objectivity comforts you. The moon does not threaten. It does not judge. It just orbits. Romeo vowed not to swear by the moon, calling it inconstant, but he was wrong. The moon is our unconditional companion. It doesn't wax and wane—the light upon it merely makes it look as if it does. We know this in our bones. And it is precisely this constancy that reaches toward us like a loving hand while we are gazing up and releases a tiny latch on the door of our souls. This is why our thoughts run deep when we are meditating under the moon.]

Now Lacy is pondering the fact that the moon she is looking at is the same moon she has gazed at through her bedroom window, the same moon under which she has written so many poems, the same moon her mother and sister could be looking at tonight. She replays her arrival in the cemetery, her struggle to understand what happened, her failure to perform during the open mic. She pictures Sam's face and wishes that he would appear and sit here with her. She wishes she would have told him how she feels about him and wonders if she'll get the chance.

After a few moments, Virginia peeks out of her grave. She gives Lacy a cold look and tiptoes over to Cumberland's crypt.

Lacy watches her calmly. Her mind is clear and she is in the mood to speak the truth.

LACY *(softly)*: I could tell on you right now.

Virginia turns, leaving one hand on the crypt door, and looks at Lacy, surprised. She quickly regains composure.

VIRGINIA: But you're not going to. I've spent a century ingratiating myself with Mrs. Steele, a strategy that has given me a certain amount of power here. I'd find a way to turn any betrayal of yours around to work against you.

LACY: Actually, you're right about the first part. I wouldn't tell on you. But it's not because I'm afraid of you, Virginia. It's because I sympathize with you.

Virginia's haughty look disappears for an instant and then she quickly slaps a cold and guarded expression back on her face.

VIRGINIA: I don't know what you mean.

Lacy stands. She has a distinct advantage over Virginia. She knows things about her, lots of things, thanks to the report she wrote on Edgar's life back in seventh grade and because of the field trip she took to their house.

LACY: You got married when you were thirteen and Edgar was twenty-seven. He was your cousin, which is weird and creepy because that's, like, illegal now, but my teacher said back then people actually did that. Anyway, thirteen is young. And my guess is that being married to Edgar wasn't such a great deal. I mean, Edgar was brilliant and original and had ambitious dreams, but he also drank and gambled. You were poor, and it was always cold, and he was always saying things would get better but they didn't. His love for you was definitely unusual, too. It was more like worship. Nobody really knows for sure, but it seems like all the two of you ever did physically was kiss, which I'm guessing was okay when you were thirteen, but maybe when you got older, you felt certain urges that Edgar couldn't fulfill and yet you were stuck married to him. I think you've found a way to survive here, but I don't think it's a way that makes you happy.

Lacy has nailed it, as she would say. Raven nods in admiration, not because he wishes to see Virginia taken down a notch. As loyal as he is to Poe, he has always felt sorry for Virginia. The reason Raven appreciates Lacy's analysis of Virginia is because it's true, and truth is something not many in Westminster dare to speak aloud.

Self-consciously, Virginia takes her hand off Cumberland's door, and Lacy continues.

LACY: I knew a girl like you in high school. She went from guy to guy to guy because it gave her something that she thought she needed, and she saw every other girl as an automatic threat, which made things worse for her because she got a reputation for being a bi—you know.

Virginia's face is a mask, but Lacy can see that she has touched a deep nerve.

VIRGINIA: You're full of theories about me.

Lacy pauses, and softens her own gaze.

LACY: I know something else about you.

VIRGINIA *(lifts her chin, trying to remain unaffected by what she's hearing)*: You do, do you?

LACY: You liked to sing.

Another flash of vulnerability passes through Virginia's eyes.

LACY: I think you had dreams of your own, Virginia Clemm Poe. I think you're lonely and unfulfilled, and I think you died way, way, way too young. I think that's sad. And I think that maybe I'm not your enemy after all.

For a moment, Virginia looks as if she might cry or drop her guard completely and say something honest to Lacy in return. But she has spent so many years perfecting the metaphoric suit of armor that she wears, she doesn't know how to act without it.

VIRGINIA *(laughing)*: You should spend more time feeling sorry for yourself, Miss Brink. I certainly don't need your pity.

She turns and slips into Cumberland's crypt.

Silence. There is a rumble of thunder in the distance, and Lacy looks toward the sound. After a few seconds, it begins to rain. Her first thought is one that she keeps to herself: Fuck. But when she realizes that the rain has no effect on her—the Dead stay dry in a deluge or a drop—she begins to laugh and she thinks: What's next?

As if answering her question, the sky opens and the rain shifts from light to absurdly drenching, and there is something about standing in the middle of the vicious downpour, something about being completely impervious to it, that gives her a feeling of power. She looks straight up, opens her arms, and chants.

LACY: I'm not going to eat termites! I'm not going to sleep away my afterlife! Or sneak around with someone I don't even like! You . . . *(she looks at Mrs. Steele's grave and raises her fist)* you are not going to win!

END OF ACT I.

INTERMISSION

A NOTE ABOUT INTERMISSION

If you are performing this as a play for the Dead, you can certainly proceed without an intermission. Regardless of how much tea we knock back, we do not require the use of lavatories, nor do we need to "stretch our legs." Free from all financial concerns, dead producers do not need to make money off concessions to defray the cost of production, either. Overall, the Dead are what you might call an easy crowd.

That said, a brief intermission can be an amusing throwback that many dead theatergoers enjoy. At the premiere of this play, we sold wine, beer, bourbon, soda, tea, and chocolate and literally charged "an arm and a leg." Hilarious. We also had male and female bathrooms; and, of course, the lines for the women's room were longer. Again, hilarious.

If you are performing this for the Living, of course, you must provide lavatories. The toilets have to actually flush. You even have to provide such amenities as sanitary products and soap. If you are in the latter group, dear Reader, I do hope that

you make enough money after all expenses have been paid to stay afloat, and my sympathies are with you.

Of course, you may be what I like to call an Armchair Enthusiast, one who enjoys reading and has no intention of producing any stage plays. In that case you may want to use the intermission to ponder what you think might happen next or which character you identify with the most. If you like, you could even discuss the philosophical questions that the work raises thus far with numerous friends and acquaintances and encourage them to purchase copies of their own. (This last morsel of advice is given not for my financial benefit, I assure you; it is merely to save you the aggravation of loaning out your own copy.)

Whatever you do during the intermission, I suggest you come back ready. There are important people here at the cemetery whom you haven't met yet, and they are dying to meet you.

ACT II

SCENE 1: SURPRISES

The rain has stopped. Occasional cracks of lightning and rumbles of departing thunder punctuate the scene as Lacy paces back and forth from the brick wall of the church to the iron gate. There and back. There and back. She has been at it for how long? An hour? Two? She can't tell. She is teetering on the edge of frustration.

In the distance, the sound of a siren can be heard. Bored, Raven mimics the sound and then he stops suddenly and looks at something with genuine surprise. An adorable Living mouse enters, completely unaware that a scene is taking place. *[Yes, dear Reader, this is completely off script!]* Without breaking character, Raven tries to get the mouse's attention so that he can gesture at it to scram. Alas, the mouse is too busy sniffing around the wet grass on the side of the church, and Raven gives up.

After a moment, the mouse stops near a tombstone, sits on its hind paws, and licks its forepaws. At the sight of something Living, Lacy brightens. She approaches it, bends down, and snaps her fingers, but it doesn't react.

LACY: Hello! *(Mouse resumes sniffing.)* You can't see me, can you? That means you're alive. If you were dead, you could see me. Rule 20 or 21: Living animals cannot see or communicate with the Dead with the exception of ravens and black cats. I read the rules, although I don't understand them. I don't understand any of it. *(Mouse finds a crumb and nibbles it.)* I had a gerbil when I was little. *(Lacy touches the mouse on the top of its head. No reaction from the creature. Another pause.)* You have no idea how lucky you are. *(Sighs)* You're alive. You're cute and free. You can scamper in and out. You can do anything—

A stray black cat leaps out from the bushes near the gate, grabs the mouse in its jaws, and carries it away. Offstage we hear the mouse's squeaks come to an abrupt and violent end.

LACY *(looks up at Raven)*: Really? Can't we have one tiny moment of enjoyment?

Raven shrugs. Lacy walks over to Poe's monument and joins the bird, slumping down with her back against the base. The fact that she can't feel how wet the ground is now makes her feel sad. Slowly she knocks her head against the marble base. Once. Twice. Three times.

LACY: It doesn't even hurt.

She does it again. Once. Twice. Three times. Above her, Raven scratches his talons against the edge. The rhythm of what he's doing combined with what she's doing creates a beat. Inspired, Lacy sits up. Her body begins to rock. The words start to flow.

LACY *(whispering)*:

I'm locked in this prison. It feels claustrophobic.
I'm stuck and I know I've got nowhere to go.
I'm surrounded by ghosts—the relics, the ancients—
supposed to have patience, supposed to just take this.

(A little louder.)
I can't get revenge. I can't disappear.
My only true friend is afraid to come near me.
I thought he'd be here. I can't blame or hate him.
How can I berate him? His fate is the same, and
the dread in this place runs as deep as a well.
Wait. This can't be heaven. So am I in he—?

She pounds out the beat, the fist of one hand into the palm of the other. Raven bobs to the rhythm.

LACY:

Look, I don't deserve this. My murderer does.
So where is the justice, the fairness? Or must I
just do what they all do and follow the order,
swallow the chore, and fall to the floor and
sleep . . .
They want us to sleep . . .
'cause the people who sleep are easy to keep
silent and meek.

(She gets up and starts to pace.)
I'm dead and my bed is a hole in the ground.
I don't want to lie down and pretend I can't see
the hypocrisy of a leader who claims to be

proper and moral and good—the whole bit—
but treats everybody around her like shi—
If we were in Salem she'd call me a witch
and put me on trial, but she is the bi—

Raven laughs. From deep beneath her feet, she feels an echo of the beat.

LACY:

Choose words wisely 'cause they don't come cheap.
But hey, there's a way to solve everything:
sleep . . .
They want us to sleep . . .
'cause the people who sleep are easy to keep
silent and meek.

Someone is listening to her. She can feel it. She runs and jumps up onto the Watson crypt roof.

LACY:

I'm so out of place, so isolated.
Those who wake up saying oh goodness gracious
with buttoned-up blouses and buttoned-up faces,
they know what their choice is. Know they can't trade places.
So what would you do? Walk a tightrope of fear
or sleep year after year?
I can't stay still. I can't be passive.
I have things to do. I have passion.

Sleep?
I can't go to sleep.

'Cause the people who sleep are easy to keep
silent and meek.
And that's not gonna be
me!

There is a moment of silence. And then a voice surprises her.

OWEN *(rising from his usual place, whispering)*: That was amazing.

Since it is not yet daybreak, Owen has been on duty, so still that Lacy hadn't noticed that he was glued to her every word.

LACY: I forgot you were here.
OWEN: I ain't heard anything like it. What was it, miss?

A male voice comes from below Lacy's feet.

EDGAR: That was poetry!

Owen and Lacy look at each other and then back down at Poe's grave.

LACY *(whispering)*: Edgar Allan Poe?

Edgar's door swings open. Another flash of lightning illuminates the graveyard. A clap of thunder follows, and a figure emerges. The man wears a black suit, crumpled and worn, with a cravat tied round his neck. He is hatless, his hair unkempt. In another flash of lightning, we see his face—the intense gaze of his dark eyes, the crooked mustache, the drooping eyebrows. It is Edgar Allan Poe.

Raven squawks softly, and Edgar looks up to see the magnificent bird on the top of his monument. He holds out his arm, as if to a dance partner, and Raven flies down to perch on it.

A shocked Owen finally speaks up, albeit in a whisper.

OWEN: You're Suppressed, sir. The likes of you ain't supposed to be up here! Please . . .

Owen feels that he should be herding Edgar back into the grave, but it doesn't seem polite to physically threaten a celebrity.

Edgar stops and looks at him, confused.

EDGAR: Wait. Where am I?
LACY: You don't know?
EDGAR: I've been asleep. I think. To tell you the truth, I can't fully remember what city I'm in. Philadelphia?
LACY: Baltimore.
EDGAR: Really? I was on my way to Philadelphia.
OWEN: You can't be up here, sir! Please . . .

Although Lacy knows that Owen will get in trouble for not enforcing the rules, she doesn't want Edgar to return to his grave.

LACY: This is your cemetery! It's Westminster.
EDGAR: I can see it's a cemetery. But what do you mean, "my" cemetery?

Lacy recognizes the look of confusion in his eyes.

LACY *(gently)*: I—I hate to break it to you, but—you're dead.
EDGAR: Dead?
LACY: I'm dead, too.

Raven lifts off Edgar's arm, flies to Poe's monument, lands on the top, and gestures down to Edgar's name.

OWEN: You died, sir, see . . . in 1849. Right after you woke up and heard what the rules are, you busted three of them, so down you went. Like I said, you can't be up here. Please . . .
EDGAR: Yes. It's coming back to me . . . *(He regards Owen from the top of his head to his boots and his eyes flash with both fear and aversion.)* I remember you, young man! I tried to make my escape a few times in those early days, and you perambulated toward me with those colossal boots. You, sir, are a nightmare.

Owen's face falls. Lacy quickly puts her hand on Owen's arm and gives him a sympathetic smile. Then she turns to Edgar.

LACY: This is Owen Hapliss. He's not a bad guy. He's just stuck in a bad job.

Since Owen has been made the Suppressor, the kind of look he is receiving from Edgar has been typical. Other than his beloved Clarissa, this Lacy girl is the only one who has ever given him a chance. He looks at Lacy, struck with gratitude.

OWEN: Thank you, miss.

EDGAR: I see. Yes, I suppose the jailor isn't evil; it is the system that creates the jailor.

He extends a hand to Owen, who, awestruck, shakes it.

OWEN *(whispering nervously)*: Thank you, sir. But . . . you have to go back down there. Now.

LACY: Can't we just let him have a little bit of freedom?

Owen has been dutiful in his job. It's all he knows. Lacy sees this and makes a different appeal.

LACY: We both know the whole Suppression thing is unfair. There are very nice people who are being Suppressed for no good reason. People like Clarissa Smythe.

Owen blushes.

LACY: How about if we work together? We let both Clarissa and Edgar out for just a few minutes and we all keep an eye out for you-know-who.

Raven flies over to Mrs. Steele's grave and nods as if to say he will help.

LACY: We will cover for each other if there are any problems. I know it's a risk, but wouldn't it be worth it?

Energy rises in Owen. His face breaks into its first smile since Clarissa became Suppressed, and we can almost hear the sad mask that has formed over his face crack.

OWEN: All right. But we keep our voices down, and if Mrs. Steele's door opens an inch, we jump right back in the grave.

EDGAR *(whispers)*: Good man.

LACY: Thank you, Owen. *(Lacy smiles.)* Go tell her!

Edgar claps Owen on the back, and Owen tiptoes to Clarissa's grave. She steps out before he can knock; she has been listening. Starry-eyed, they kiss.

Lacy turns to Edgar.

LACY: You really do have to dive if Mrs. Steele wakes up.

EDGAR: Mrs. Steele! There's a woman one can't forget! *(Turns to Lacy)* And you are?

LACY: I'm Lacy Brink. I'm what they call a Modern.

EDGAR: What century?

LACY: The twenty-first century.

EDGAR *(bowing slightly)*: Your poem woke me up. I can't say I understood all the references but I appreciate your use of rhythm and rhyme.

LACY: Thank you. I mean, that's an amazing thing to hear coming from Edgar Allan Poe.

EDGAR *(a giddy look coming into his eyes)*: Wait! You're a Modern and yet you know me. That must mean . . .

LACY: You're famous.

Edgar leans jauntily against his monument, inhales dramatically, and speaks in the most sonorous and spine-chilling whisper imaginable:

EDGAR:

"On this home by Horror haunted—tell me truly,
I implore—
Is there—is there balm in Gilead?—tell me—tell me,
I implore!"
Quoth the Raven—

RAVEN *(puffs up and squawks softly)*: Nevermore!

EDGAR: Ha!

LACY: That's from your poem "The Raven." We read it in my seventh-grade English class. We went to see your house and came here to see your grave. I wrote a whole report on you. I've been coming here to write poems ever since.

Lacy pauses. She was going to say that it was weird of her to be such a fan considering how old-fashioned his work was. To be honest, she couldn't get through some of it. But then she realized that, when so many of those long-ago writers were writing about the beauty of a rose or of a sunset, Edgar probably appealed to her because he did the opposite. He was preoccupied by things like the agony of grief and the torture of guilt, of a tell-tale heart that keeps beating after a murder, of a black cat that haunts the drunk man who killed it, of pits with pendulums, of insanity. He explored the mysteries of passions and he acknowledged that there is a dark side to human nature, which is the most disturbing mystery of all.

[I beg of you, dear Reader, to indulge me for another quick aside. If you are a young adult reading this book, I'd like to acknowledge that it can be challenging to comprehend or even

grasp the relevance of the writing of a different period or culture or style than one's own but, in trying, one's horizon is expanded in ways that are not immediately apparent. A reader of literature becomes a citizen not only of the world, but also, more importantly, of time—not geologic time, which is certainly magnificent, but human time, the only time that is aware of itself—and since literature is primarily the result of passion and insight, a reader of literature learns the deepest passions and insights that have moved people across time. This knowledge has a way of seeping into the soul and ultimately nourishing it. Think of each work of literature as an individual raindrop that is trickling into the soil. From the outside the ground may look dry, but those nourishing drops have sunk far beneath the surface and are ready to be pulled in by the roots of the tree, to be carried up the trunk, and to be lifted into leaves.

If you are not a young adult, but instead are one of those most intrepid souls—a teacher, librarian, or bookseller reading works to determine the merit of recommendation—I say, huzzah and thank you! Books that have complex sentence structures, poetic language, thought-provoking themes—or absurdly long asides to the reader—benefit greatly from your energy and enthusiasm. I do hope you are enjoying this one.

And now, back to our story.]

EDGAR: I'm famous! Isn't this wonderful? A dream come true!

Edgar takes Lacy by the hands and begins twirling with her. Raven puffs up with pleasure. Lacy laughs and looks back at Owen, who is caught up in a tender conversation with Clarissa. She spins out of the dance and catches her breath.

LACY: I guess it feels good to find out you're famous.

EDGAR *(stops and looks at Lacy thoughtfully)*: It sounds so superficial to desire fame. But . . . fame . . . it isn't such a purely superficial thing . . . is it? Fame is a sign, the proof that what you've created will live forever. That's what I really wanted. For things of complex beauty to . . . live. Is it so terrible to want beautiful things to last? Is it so terrible to do anything to try and make it happen? A thing of beauty shouldn't die! Every woman I loved died—my mother, my stepmother, my wife—and there was nothing I could do to stop it. The flesh perishes, but a poem can have eternal life! Long after your beloved dies, you can hold a poem about your beloved and breathe it in and experience its tender embrace.

LACY: That was beautiful.

EDGAR: The truth is beautiful. *(Suddenly extremely excited)* Perhaps you know how I died, Miss Brink! I'm recalling that when I was inducted into this place, I wanted to know how I perished, and no one seemed to know. I was overcome with paroxysms of frustration and I cried out several times, using words that were, I admit, most profane.

LACY: That's why you got three strikes? See, that's what pi— *(She leans in and lowers her voice.)* That's what pisses me off. Sometimes people swear when they're angry. You shouldn't get Suppressed for that!

EDGAR: Do you know how I died?

LACY: I wrote about that in my report. It was very interesting. Everyone says that you died under mysterious circumstances.

Edgar pulls Lacy over to sit on the stone bench.

EDGAR: I love mysterious circumstances! Tell me more!

LACY: You were in Richmond collecting subscriptions for a new magazine that you wanted to publish. Things were looking up. You were in good spirits. You wrote a letter to Mrs. Clemm—

EDGAR: Muddy!

LACY: Yes, your nickname for Maria. You wrote a letter to Muddy explaining that you were going to Philadelphia to edit a collection of poems for which you were being paid. Before leaving, you visited a Dr. Carter.

EDGAR: Yes, John Carter! I remember his cane . . . loved it! Wanted one for myself. It had a hidden sword in it!

LACY: Yes. Well, you seem to have mistaken his cane for yours because you left with it that day.

EDGAR: Really? *(Leans in, whispering)* Do you think I did it on purpose?

LACY: I don't know. No one knows.

EDGAR: So I filched his cane and then what?

LACY: For some unknown reason, you didn't go to Philadelphia. You came here instead.

EDGAR: Baltimore . . .

LACY: Yes. Accounts differ on what you did here, but several days after your arrival, you were found delirious and destitute, wandering around in someone else's clothing.

EDGAR *(leaning back on the bench, fairly swooning with the drama)*: What in God's name happened to me?

LACY: No one knows for certain. Some say you were drunk, others say you had been robbed and suffered a beating!

EDGAR: A beating! *(He pulls up his sleeves to check for bruises.)*

LACY: Another theory is that you were kidnapped by a gang to be used as a straw voter in a local election.

EDGAR: No!

LACY: Yes, as the story goes, the gang tortured you and forced you to vote for their candidate and then tossed you out onto the street.

EDGAR: Like a common sack of trash? A crime! Murder by a mob!

LACY: But there are other theories, too.

EDGAR *(delighted)*: More? How else might I have perished?

LACY: Congestion of the brain, heart disease, tuberculosis, diabetes, epilepsy, carbon monoxide poisoning . . . rabies . . .

EDGAR *(standing up to dance with a perversely impish joy at the list)*: Rabies! Fantastic! Perhaps I was visited by a bat in my sleep. Whilst I lay, the thing sank its fangs into my pale and throbbing neck. And then?

LACY *(laughing)*: Wow. I'm amazed that you're having so much fun with this. I'm not exactly taking the news of my death as well.

EDGAR *(leaning in to whisper with a crazy grin)*: I'm Edgar Allan Poe. Master of the Macabre. Guru of the Ghoulish. Writer of the Warped. Sultan of the Strange. Tell me more!

LACY: You were taken to the hospital, where you lapsed in and out of consciousness.

EDGAR *(sprawling on a nearby sarcophagus as if on his deathbed)*: No doubt, saying things of both profound beauty and utter incoherence! Who paid me a visit?

LACY: I'm sure many tried. I believe you were deemed to be too excitable. On October 7, 1849, you took your last breath.

EDGAR: And what were my dying words?

LACY: People disagree.

EDGAR: Really? What are the choices?

LACY *(counting them off on her fingers)*: One: "Lord help my poor soul." Two: "He who arched the heavens and upholds the universe, has His decrees legibly written upon the frontlet of every human being." Three: "Herring."

EDGAR: Definitely the second.

LACY: Definitely.

EDGAR: Well, I love it! Wonderful tale! I am exceedingly obliged, Miss Brink. And now here I am in the flesh. Ha! I suppose I can't say that. I should say "in the—" *(He looks down at his body.)* What shall we call this? "In the corpse" doesn't sound poetic enough. Ugly word, *corpse.*

LACY: Here in the spirit?

EDGAR: The spectre?

LACY: The ghostly shade?

EDGAR: The phantasm?

LACY: The otherworldly presence?

EDGAR: The vapor? Even better. The bloodless vapor!

LACY: How about the supernatural shadow?

EDGAR: The gauzy illusion?

LACY: The ethereal essence?

EDGAR: The astral nature!

LACY: The imponderable being.

EDGAR: Lovely.

LACY *(beaming)*: Thank you.

EDGAR: Ah! The bracing tonic of words. Words give us the strength to face the ignoble vagaries; the poison-tipped arrows; the petty, shallow foibles of existence. How could I have stayed abed so long? Let us not waste another moment. Let us conspire to share more poetry!

Enthusiasm vibrates out from Edgar, zipping around the cemetery like a fresh spring breeze. Lacy wants to encourage it, but she can't ignore the reality of their situation.

LACY: I tried to have an open mic—a night of poetry—and it su—it didn't go well. Mrs. Steele scared everybody away.

EDGAR: A night of poetry! We must do it.

LACY: But you're Suppressed. Even if I talked my way into doing another one, you wouldn't be allowed to be there. *(Getting up from her bench)* Unless—

EDGAR: Miss Brink, I see a veritable spark of mischief in your eyes. What are you thinking?

Lacy waves at Owen to come over. Cautiously, he keeps one eye on Mrs. Steele's grave and tiptoes over with Clarissa to join them. Whispered introductions are made and then Lacy lays out her idea.

LACY *(whispering)*: I'm thinking . . . what if we could find a way to get rid of Mrs. Steele for an hour or two? Then we could have a real open mic. The other people here . . . I know they need it.

EDGAR: Let's do it! We could stuff old Mrs. Steele under the floorboards or brick her up in a catacomb. *(He notices the shocked expressions.)* Ha! I jest! Of course, we can't murder her. She's already dead!

LACY: How deep are the catacombs? If we found some reason for her to be way, way down there with the door closed, could she hear us, Owen?

OWEN: Not unless you screamed your loudest. If you could find a way to get her down there, I could watch the door, miss.

LACY: Thank you, Owen.

EDGAR: Let's devise a hoax. I've always loved a good hoax.
LACY: Edgar has to be allowed to attend the open mic. Actually, maybe we should allow all the Suppressed to attend.

Clarissa's eyes light up. Owen takes this in.

LACY: I know it's a huge risk. If we get caught, we'll all be in trouble. If you don't want—
OWEN: I think we should do it.

Clarissa hugs him, and Lacy grins.

SCENE 2: THE SECRET PLAN

A rustling in the vicinity of Mrs. Steele's grave sends Poe and Clarissa running, but when the cat appears and then slinks off, they stop and return.

The sky has that fragile look it gets before dawn. The moon, large and low, is sinking on the horizon.

OWEN *(whispering)*: This is dangerous. It's nearing daybreak. Peter will be making his rounds soon.

LACY: Let's at least wake the core group and tell them the plan tonight while Mrs. Steele is asleep. I'm thinking Sam, Sarah, Billy, Dr. Hosler, the Spindly Sisters, Peter, Maria. *(She glances at Cumberland's crypt.)* I'm just not sure if Virginia—

Momentarily forgetting about Edgar, Lacy was going to say that she wasn't sure if Virginia could be trusted, but at the mention of his wife, Edgar spins around and looks at her name on the side of his monument.

EDGAR: Virginia!

LACY and OWEN: Sshh!

Owen begs both Clarissa and Edgar to return to their graves. Clarissa does. Edgar is too agitated. While Owen runs back to keep a closer eye on Mrs. Steele's grave, Edgar whispers rapturously.

EDGAR: Oh, my mind and heart have been shrouded in the excitement or I would have instantly called out for my love. My love that was loved with a love that was more than love! My eternal bride! I cannot express in words the fervent devotion I feel. If I could not be with her I would not wish to live another hour—Virginia! Virginia, darling! *(He runs to the side of the monument that bears her name.)*

LACY *(whispering)*: Keep it down! Um—I think she is *(she gives a sideways glance at Cumberland's crypt)* . . . maybe . . . on a stroll. I'm sure she'll be back soon. Let's go get Sam first.

Owen waves to stop her. He points to Sam's grave and then to Mrs. Steele's, making the point that the proximity makes it too risky to wake Sam at the moment. Lacy nods. She'll wake the others first and find a way to tell Sam when it's safe.

For extra insurance, Lacy convinces Edgar to return to his grave.

One by one, Lacy wakes Sarah, Dr. Hosler, the Spindly sisters, Peter, and Maria. As each person rises, the plan is introduced to much surprise and a fair amount of initial apprehension. We hear none of the actual dialogue, but we can tell by the excitement that something fundamental is shifting for these residents. Now that Lacy is tempting them with the idea of a colorful evening without the dreaded Mrs. Steele, they can't go back to the drab gray of fear. Maria, in particular, is eager to see her dear Eddy again. They debate about whether to include Virginia and Cumberland. Maria insists that Virginia can be trusted, but they decide to wait until she comes out of the Poltroon crypt. They think it's best to leave Cumberland out.

Lacy fleshes out the hoax. They have dreamed up an excuse to send Mrs. Steele to the catacombs, but they will need a volunteer to help keep her there for at least an hour or two. Although no one wants to miss the evening, when Dr. Hosler sees the looks of joyful anticipation on the faces of the younger people, he raises his hand to volunteer.

DR. HOSLER: I'll do it. I had a full and happy life, which I know some of you weren't lucky enough to have.

Lacy kisses him on the cheek, and his eyes grow moist.

DR. HOSLER: I . . . I . . . forgot how sweet that feels.
LACY: Don't tell me there's a rule against kissing your friend.
EFFIE *(whispering)*: There isn't a rule, per se, but we've developed a habit of keeping to ourselves.
NEFFIE: The atmosphere here hasn't been conducive to physical signs of affection.
BILLY: If I'd a-known there'd be a kiss, I'd have volunteered myself.

Effie and Neffie giggle.

EFFIE: Perhaps kisses should be volunteered for any number of reasons, Mr. Bodley.
NEFFIE: Or no reason at all!

Just as Effie and Neffie's giggle encourages Billy to become bolder in his flirtation, Sam is waking up.

Usually quick to rise, it had taken Sam so long to fall asleep, he is now off his timing. The moment he opens his eyes, his thoughts are on Lacy and Billy. Did they spend the night together? Are the looks Lacy gives to Billy the looks of a friend or something more? How does one tell? He has the panicky thought that Billy will not be his only rival. What he loves about Lacy—the fact that she has affection and passionate concern for others—is also what challenges and confuses him. But maybe all his worries are for naught, he thinks. Maybe he can win her heart after all.

[And here, dear Reader, is where we have one of those moments that we wish we could prevent.]

While Sam is talking himself into rising, Billy is pouncing on Neffie's playful innuendo and is making a game, first of kissing Effie on the cheek and then progressing to Neffie and then . . . you can guess where this is heading.

At the moment that Sam rises and peeks out, Billy plants a kiss upon Lacy's cheek.

Sam reels back.

Lacy laughs, whispers something to Billy, and gathers the others closer to her. Billy at her elbow, she is holding court in a warm, happy huddle, with a smile on her face. The hope Sam had been trying to nurture boils into despair.

LACY: Okay, does everybody understand the plan?

DR. HOSLER: I will do everything in my power to keep her in the catacombs for as long as possible.

A plan . . . ? Sam tiptoes out and hides behind a tombstone to hear.

MARIA: The only way this will work is if no one betrays us.
EFFIE: What about Samuel?

Sam freezes.

OWEN: We can't wake him up. He's too close. Too risky.

The fact that Owen is a part of this clique adds to Sam's pain.

MARIA: I don't think we should include him in the open mic. He is her son.
DR. HOSLER: Perhaps it would strengthen the ruse to make him part of it. As her son, he could be invited to the catacombs with her.
EFFIE: Very reasonable.
NEFFIE: Kill two birds with one stone, really.

Raven growls, and Neffie apologizes.

Sam has heard enough. He walks to his grave.

Ordinarily Raven's affection for Sam would compel him to do something for Sam, cough loudly in his direction so everyone would see him and have the chance for explanations and apologies, for example; but Raven is a bird, after all, and Neffie's comment about the stone rankles. And so, as any tragedy would have it, while Raven growls at Neffie, Sam descends out of sight, missing what Lacy says next.

LACY: But I don't want Sam to miss the open mic.
SARAH: I think his feelings would be deeply hurt.
EFFIE: He needn't know. He wouldn't read anyway. *(She nods toward the urn holding Sam's crumpled poetry.)*
NEFFIE: He discards his attempts.
EFFIE: It takes courage to perform.
LACY: But it won't be the same without him.
DR. HOSLER: I sympathize with the boy, but minimizing the risk for us all is the best option.

Raven hears a sound at Mrs. Steele's grave and flaps a warning.

Quickly Lacy sits on her bench and Owen steps into the shadows by the wall. Everybody else begins to saunter aimlessly in different directions.

Mrs. Steele's door opens fully. She steps out of her grave and looks at the strange sight.

MRS. STEELE: It's almost daybreak. I heard talking. What in the world is everyone doing walking around?

Nonchalantly, Raven lifts one wing and uses the wing tip to scratch the back of his head. Knowing it is best for the group if she is out of sight, Lacy dives into her grave.

MARIA *(thinking fast)*: We were feeling restless, Mrs. Steele . . .

She looks at the Spindly sisters for help, and they jump in.

EFFIE: We couldn't sleep and . . . and . . .

NEFFIE: Dr. Hosler gave us an exercise! *(She looks expectantly at Dr. Hosler.)*

DR. HOSLER *(panics for a moment and then recovers)*: An old remedy. It clears the mind and relaxes the muscles. Here we go. Counting off. One and two and three and four . . .

Dr. Hosler ad-libs a slow yogic dance of sorts, counting as he goes, taking a step with his right foot, lifting his other foot in the air, and reaching up with his arms, and then repeating the whole with his other foot moving forward. The others join in, continuing to count and step and lift and reach. In the dark underground, Lacy listens, imagining the comedic movements, hoping Mrs. Steele buys the excuse, and trying not to laugh.

NEFFIE *(continuing to do the routine)*: It's a bit mesmerizing. I am feeling sleepy. Aren't you, Effie?

EFFIE: I am. It's a bit like . . . counting sheep . . . only physical.

MARIA *(yawning with one hand as she reaches up with the other)*: I shall sleep like a baby after this. I can feel it.

Mrs. Steele is silent for a moment, regarding them with suspicion, as they continue.

MRS. STEELE: You all felt restless at the same time?

DR. HOSLER: Full moon, Mrs. Steele. Scientists have long hypothesized that the lunar phases influence sleep patterns, most specifically the association of insomnia with the full moon. *(He grins, enjoying this little opportunity to lecture again.)* Anecdotal evidence has existed for hundreds of years, which is why we have the word *lunatic.*

The group is into it now, counting and dancing. Mrs. Steele walks between them, looking for Lacy. She has the distinct feeling that the girl has something to do with all this, but Lacy seems to have gone to sleep.

MRS. STEELE: I don't like this. I am not a medical doctor, but I can't see how this . . . this ridiculous dancing about can bring forth anything but agitation. *(She notices Peter among them.)* Peter Brown! You, too? You're never up before it's time for daybreak.

PETER: Actually, it is almost time for daybreak. I was just about to do my rounds, ma'am. *(He pulls out his bell.)* Oyez! Oyez! Daybreak in five.

MRS. STEELE *(relieved to have a sound excuse to send everyone to bed)*: You heard him! Daybreak.

Disgusted with the lot, Mrs. Steele returns to her grave.

The group holds its collective breath, looking at each other to make sure she is really gone, and then Lacy's and Edgar's heads pop out of their graves with huge smiles, and they all burst into grins. Lacy gives a thumbs-up to Dr. Hosler, the Spindly sisters, and Maria for being so devious and fast on their feet.

LACY *(whispering)*: Everyone get to bed. We'll start our plan at midnight tomorrow!

The group begins heading to their graves, when the door to the Poltroon crypt opens. Virginia peeks out, as she usually does when she hears Peter's warning, to see if

the coast is clear of Mrs. Steele so that she can safely return to her grave.

Edgar sees her pretty face and cries out.

EDGAR: My love!

Immediately, Mrs. Steele's door flings open. Edgar and Lacy duck back down into their graves. Virginia shrinks back into Cumberland's crypt and shuts the door quickly from the inside.

MRS. STEELE: What was that?

Dr. Hosler realizes that a man's voice is needed, and so he pretends to be finishing the routine.

DR. HOSLER *(performing the routine)*: Reach above and step! Just finishing the count, Mrs. Steele. Off to bed now, everyone.

As everyone returns to their graves, Mrs. Steele does the same.

Lacy peeks out, trying to decide if she should try to get Edgar's attention and somehow warn him about Virginia's tendency to . . . well, roam, but Edgar doesn't give her a chance. He opens his door and tiptoes out to whisper at Cumberland's crypt.

EDGAR: Virginia? Are you in there, my darling?

The crypt door opens and Virginia sheepishly steps out. All we see of Cumberland is his pale, nervous hand,

pulling the crypt door closed. Edgar envelops Virginia and she fakes a smile.

VIRGINIA: Eddy. You're Suppressed. How can you be up?
EDGAR: I have allies, Virginia! *(He waves at Lacy and Owen.)* Isn't it wonderful? Oh how I've missed you! Wait . . . what were you doing in Cumberland Poltroon's crypt?
VIRGINIA: Of course it was empty. I went in to borrow . . . a handkerchief. But no one was home. Absolutely no one.

It's a ridiculous lie. Doesn't make a bit of sense. But Edgar is too excited to see through it.

EDGAR: Come! We have exciting plans. I'll tell you the abridged version, darling. We don't have much time.

As Edgar whispers the plan to Virginia, she turns and looks at Lacy.

Much can be accurately read into a look and much can be projected. Lacy sees annoyance. Virginia has no desire to play wife and the waking up of Edgar is presenting a problem that she'll have to solve. But there is also admiration for Lacy in Virginia's look. Lacy's plan is ambitious. The waking up of energy . . . Virginia has been craving this. She'll be an ally, Lacy thinks, although she'll be jealous and prickly. The open mic will be something she won't want to miss.

Peter finishes his rounds and descends into his grave. The ritual countdown begins.

ALL: Ten, nine, eight . . .

Virginia and Edgar descend.

On his way to his own grave on the other side of the church, Owen catches Lacy's eye and gives her a nod and a smile.

Lacy returns it, but the happy feeling catches in her throat. She looks to Sam's grave, missing him. When they can emerge again, she will convince the others to include him. She can't have an open mic without Sam.

[Speaking of poor Sam, you're probably wondering about him, dear Reader. Take a look. He is face down in his grave, hands covering his ears, seething with anger at his friends for leaving him out and at himself for being too timid to speak. Even in this ultimate privacy, he chokes back his tears instead of letting them go.]

ALL: Seven, six, five, four, three, two . . .

Raven flies back to his perch on Poe's monument. There is one last violent crack of lightning and . . .

BLACKOUT.

SCENE 3: SOUNDTRACK OF ANOTHER ORDINARY DAY

The Dead are sleeping—even Lacy. We begin again in darkness, which is pregnant and familiar, and we sit on the edges of our seats, listening . . . waiting . . .

Gradually we hear the soft chirping of morning bird-song, the far-off whir of a car, and then the slow crescendo of a city street waking up.

As the sky lightens, the cemetery and the street beyond its iron gate take on colors as if the world is being dyed before our eyes, growing more vibrant with each passing second.

Amid the increasing sonic traffic, we hear footsteps and an argument between a homeless man and a business owner. Obscenities stab the air. The horn from a pass-ing car blares into prominence and then fades. We hear another person passing by, possibly mentally ill, singing a song of exuberance. For a few seconds it fills the space and then drifts away.

Morning rolls by. Noon brings tourists, laughter, and music. At some point, a bus rolls up, the door sighs open, and immediately, there is the clatter and scuffling of a school group getting off.

For a few moments the cemetery is all chaos and

cacophony as thirty-three middle-school students spread out like a virus. The teacher's voice competes for attention. They have already been to Poe's sad, claustrophobic house on Amity Street; this is their last stop, and the teacher is exhausted.

She begins a recitation of the history of Westminster, the name *Poe* rising to the surface over and over like the whitecap of a wave.

After a while, the school group floats away and eventually we hear the sighing of the bus door and the rolling away of the tires.

Late afternoon settles down like a nap, and then there is a burst of activity at rush hour. The sounds build and then lower in intensity and volume as another day draws to a close.

Again, Owen and Clarissa emerge for their secret rendezvous. Her face glows. He wants to walk over and take her in his arms, but he reminds himself to be patient. They whisper *I love you* and descend back to sleep.

Time passes. In the late evening, we hear the distinct creak of the iron gate, and once again the hairs on the back of our necks stand at attention. The sound of footsteps on crunching leaves betrays the Living. In the moonlight, we see Olivia enter.

She stops and looks up at Poe's monument. Perched on top, Raven regards her, unmoving.

Olivia bends down and picks up a stone. She throws it at the bird, who doesn't flinch, and then she laughs when it misses by a long margin. In the next second, her cell phone vibrates in her coat pocket and she ignores it, sitting on the stone bench.

OLIVIA *(looking around the cemetery)*: This place sucks. Sorry, Lacy. I know you liked it. *(She pauses.)* Mom didn't know that. I mentioned it to her when we were talking about your ashes and she said, "What cemetery?" And I said, "The Poe cemetery. You know how she went there all the time to write her poems?" She got quiet and then she went into the bathroom and closed the door. I could hear her puking. I think she was sick to her stomach that she didn't know this basic thing about you, Lacy. Then she came out and smiled and said, "That's a good idea," like nothing was wrong.

At the sound of her name, Lacy wakes up. Immediately, she rises to peer out, knowing now to stay halfway in. Although she thinks she is prepared, the vividness of her sister's face in close proximity catches her off guard.

Olivia is looking down with eyes that see only dirt. She's wearing Zane's coat and jeans and her red fleece gloves, the ones whose tips she cut off last year. Her legs are bouncing slightly to keep warm. Her nose is running and she keeps dragging the back of one gloved hand across her face.

OLIVIA: A week ago, I woke up at around three or four in the morning and I heard breathing. And I could just feel this living presence behind the curtain, you know, and I was fucking terrified, like you were back but not in a good way. Like it was some fucking horror movie. And I lifted the curtain and it wasn't you. It was Mom. She was sleeping in your bed. It still freaked me out. I slept on the couch and when I woke up neither of us talked about it. She hasn't done it since.

LACY: A week ago? How long have I been dead?

Disturbed, Lacy looks at Raven, who shifts slightly as if trying to decide whether to explain. Lacy can see in his eyes that it's true. She has been dead longer than she thought. How long, she doesn't know. She recalls Effie saying that it took Edgar weeks to rise. Perhaps it's different for every person. She turns her attention back to her sister, determined not to miss the chance to hear more.

As it happens, that slight movement of Raven has made Olivia turn to look at him. She and the bird lock eyes.

Breathlessly, Lacy watches her sister stare at the bird, not wanting to blink, wishing she could open the door to her sister's mind and hear what she's thinking.

[Unlike her, dear Reader, you have the benefit of an omniscient narrator, so you can lean forward now and hear what Lacy cannot.]

A thought occurs to Olivia, the way thoughts do: suddenly, mysteriously. She'd like to change places with the bird. Be some emotionless, solitary creature, accountable for and to no one.

Raven remains silent.

Olivia turns away, looks up at the moon. The painkiller she took about half an hour ago, the second to last one from the prescription bottle she stole out of the medicine cabinet at Zane's dad's house, is starting to kick in. It will melt one area inside her—a zone that runs from the base of her skull all the way down the back of her legs—but, mixed with the vodka, it will make her stomach ache; and she knows that neither the drug nor the booze will be able to soften the cold, hard shell that now defines her. Ever since Lacy's death, it has felt like something physiological has happened to her: her top layer of skin has fused with her body's chi, or whatever that energy is called that is always supposed to be flowing just under the skin, and it has hardened like a coating. I am bitter and brittle, and this is my new life, she thinks.

She digs the fingernails of her left hand into her left cheek, which she does now and then, just to see if she still has any feeling left in her skin. Is she pressing hard? Does it hurt? She can't tell.

A shiver runs through her. There is no wind, but the cold is intensifying.

OLIVIA: Everything is hard. Going to sleep is hard. Waking up is hard. School is . . . fucking impossible. I couldn't go today. I went to Crimmson's Café.

A sudden image comes to Olivia. She is sitting on her bed and Lacy is tucked into her own bed, listening through the curtain. Just as the image begins to comfort her, it dissolves.

OLIVIA: I sat at the table you like, the one outside, even though it was kind of cold. And I ordered your favorite . . . cinnamon crumb cake. I bet you didn't think I remembered.

Olivia laughs, but it comes out choked. Lacy holds her breath.

OLIVIA: It was the waitress with the big hair. Remember when we went there with Mom on Valentine's Day and that song came on the restaurant's playlist and the three of us started singing really softly and then the waitress came over and sang really loudly with us? That one.

Lacy remembers. It was last year. She and Olivia had surprised their mom by taking her out to dinner and paying for it with their own money. The waitress had told them all that they were as cute as peas in a pod, which their mom had loved.

OLIVIA: Anyway, I don't think the waitress remembered that because it was just me sitting there. She brings the cake, and I say thanks, and . . . I can't eat it. She comes back after a while and says, "Is there something wrong with it?" And I say no . . . nothing's wrong . . . and I smile at her and she smiles back and she pours a little more water into my glass and walks to the next table. And the cake is sitting there on the plate. A perfect piece. A middle piece, which I know is exactly what you like, and it's a big piece, a lucky one, perfectly baked, not too brown, with just the right amount of crumbles on the top. And it smells so good. It smells really fucking delicious, Lacy.

It hurts Olivia to talk, as if something bitter is expanding in her throat, but she keeps going. Lacy blinks back tears. She wants to climb out and put her arms around her sister, but she doesn't move.

OLIVIA: And then the waitress comes by again and she says, "Really, if there's something wrong, I can take it back." And I smile and I say, "It's fine. I just ordered it for someone else." And she says, "Oh," and she brings another glass of water to the table, assuming someone else is on their way. And now the glass of water is sitting there with the cake and the empty chair. And then after a while she comes by again and says, “Can I get you anything else?” And I say no thanks, just the check. And she says, “Do you want to take that home?” And the word *home* does something funny to me. It kind of stabs me and I can’t talk so I nod and she gives me a to-go box and the check and walks away. And I open the to-go box and time shifts into slow motion. For a few seconds, I’m just looking at this open box, which is waiting for the cake. And then when I pick up the piece of cake to put it in, the body of the cake feels so perfect. It doesn’t fall apart or break. It holds its shape, and it’s like I’m picking up a little baby, and I’m setting it in the box, and the way it feels when I let go and the cake comes to a rest in the box is killing me. It fits perfectly in the box and it’s killing me, Lacy. I have to close the fucking lid and I just sit there and stare at it.

Olivia closes her eyes tight, and Lacy can hear her breath coming in shallow bits.

OLIVIA: Goddamn it, Lacy. I need a drink.

Olivia gets up.

LACY: Liv . . . don’t.

In his grave, Sam feels the tension of Lacy’s distress, her thwarted desire for her sister to stay. He wakes up and looks out.

An image comes to Lacy unbidden. It is the night she wanted to go to the open mic at Tenuto's. She is standing in the kitchen, arguing with Olivia.

LACY: We had a fight that night . . . didn't we, Liv? Mom texted you and said you had to drive me to school and you got mad.

The image of the two of them in the kitchen becomes fuzzy. Lacy tries to grab the memory, but it disappears.

LACY: No . . . that can't be right . . . I wasn't going to school that night.

Lacy is sure that if Olivia stays, more of her own memory will come back, but Olivia walks to the gate.

LACY: Liv . . .

Lacy doesn't move, but her soul reaches out with such longing, Lacy feels as if something inside her is going to break.

Sam is about to whisper Lacy's name, when Billy rises from his grave. Billy looks to see if Mrs. Steele is up and sees Sam peering out. Quickly Billy jumps out of his grave and goes to Lacy before Sam moves. Ashamed, Sam ducks underground.

BILLY: Are you all right?
LACY: You shouldn't be out.
BILLY: I heard you. What can I do?

LACY: Go back, Billy. I don't want to get you in trouble. I'm going, too.

Lacy looks at Sam's grave, hoping to see his face. Billy is attentive, but it's Sam she needs. Reluctantly she returns underground. Billy returns to his grave.

High overhead there is a helicopter sound. The last light of the evening fades.

After several long minutes, Sam emerges halfway. It isn't midnight yet. He looks out at the quiet graveyard, wondering if Lacy is sleeping, if she's alone.

He takes out his pencil and journal and writes without stopping.

Dear Lacy,

Fear is a crippling disease. It has paralyzed my feet when I should have stepped forward. It has withered my hand when I should have reached for yours. Yet fear is also the firm push at my back. If I don't act now, I will forever regret my cowardice, and we both know what forever means.

Three days ago when the bells tolled, I woke, believing that the night would unfold as all the others had, and then Raven spoke your name. How conflicted I was, for your arrival brought immediate joy to me and sorrow to you. With every passing second, my affection for you grew. How, in such a short time, can feelings blossom so? Truthfully, I do not know. All I know is that my love for you feels miraculous—a garden springing from a parched desert.

Yes . . . I will say it . . . I love you, Lacy.

Is this confession wise or ridiculous? I cannot begin to parse it. The attention from Billy Bodley and your sweet gazes back at him have robbed me of any confidence; and yet, here I am, revealing my heart to you.

And now I must also confess that I eavesdropped on your plan to host an open mic with the others. If I were alive I would say that it is killing me to be excluded. Yes, I am a Steele. But I thought that you, Lacy, would see into my heart and know the truth: that I despise the Steele yoke that I was born to bear, that I long to be free of it, and that I would never betray you.

My hope is that a seed of love for me is tucked in the folds of your heart and that my words will nourish the garden within you. If nothing else, perhaps my admission will release the pressure in my chest, for so powerful is my love for you, my heart threatens to burst.

Please give me a chance.

But do not think that my thoughts are only for myself. In addition to telling you of my love, I want to tell you that my thoughts are with you. I am sorry for your homesickness. I am sorry for the pain of not understanding how you died. I am sorry for the heartbreak that you experience when your sister comes. I know how hard it must be to see her and not be able to communicate with her.

If I were a magician and could turn your pain into a shape, I would form it into a termite that I would gladly swallow for you.

You may not be able to believe me, but I believe that your pain will lessen with time. Your soul is too buoyant and beautiful to stay mired. In time, you will heal. And I want to do everything in my power to help speed you into a happier embrace.

With eternal love,
Sam

Sam sits back, surprised at himself. Raven nods. After a breath, Sam rolls the letter tightly and holds it out. Raven flies down and takes it in one claw. As soon as the great bird lifts into the air, Sam winces but doesn't call him back. Raven lands on Lacy's grave, pokes the small cylinder of paper into the earth, and flies back to Poe's monument.

Just the tip of the paper is visible above the ground. Sam watches and waits, imagining Lacy in her grave looking up and pulling the letter in to read. Minutes pass and the paper remains untouched, for Lacy has fallen asleep. Knowing there is nothing more he can do, Sam sighs and returns to his coffin.

Even Raven settles down on top of Poe's monument, tucks his head under one wing, and closes his eyes.

[The dark silence ticks, but look carefully, dear Reader, just beyond Lacy's grave. If you are observant, you will see what Sam—and even Raven—did not notice: the door to Billy's grave is raised a crack. Billy has been watching.]

Quietly, Billy emerges, tiptoes to Lacy's grave, grasps the protruding tip of the letter, and pulls it out. Raven looks. Billy, seeing Raven's movement out of the corner of his eye, turns his back to the bird and secretly pops the letter into his mouth. As he walks back to his own grave, he chews and swallows every bit.

SCENE 4: HOAXES

How many souls are turning in their graves? At the moment, our hearts are with one: poor unsuspecting Sam, tossing in his grave, innocently waiting to see if his beloved will offer sweet reciprocation of a letter she will not even receive. Just before midnight he finally falls into a deep sleep.

Now the bells begin to toll, and Lacy is waking. It is the third midnight here at Westminster, and what Dr. Hosler said in scene 2 about how quickly we adapt to our circumstances is true. Lacy continues to have questions about her death and concern for those she left behind, but the midnight bells have tolled and there are people and things here to deal with.

She hops out of her grave. The sky is clear of clouds. The glowing moon appears as if a stage manager has just pulled off the gray silk that had been draping it. Lacy's mind is clear too, and, thinking of Sam, she races to his grave. Not daring to knock for fear of waking his mother, she sees that he has left his satchel out. She can leave him a message. He'll be thrilled to discover it. From it she pulls his pencil and paper. Hastily she writes a note:

Dear Sam,

We have a plan for a new open mic. I want you there but don't have time to give you all the details. An announcement is going to be made about your mom winning a fake award and you'll be included in the invitation to a ceremony in the catacombs. Make up an excuse to stay here. Don't worry. I'll explain everything and convince the others. I have been missing you! I need you. Love, Lacy

It feels good to write this note. Sam's absence has been bothering Lacy. We are elated, too, believing that there is hope for Sam after all.

But a sound changes everything. Billy, having crept behind Lacy, clears his throat.

Lacy turns, note in hand.

BILLY *(whispers with a smile)*: There you are! I couldn't wait to see you. *(He looks at the note in her hand and quickly pulls her away from the Steele plots.)* Come where we won't have to whisper.

Lacy can feel his interest in her, and she wants to tell him that as much as she appreciates the attention, she has feelings for Sam. But before she can speak, the regulars rise, earlier than usual—Owen, Sarah, the Spindly sisters, Dr. Hosler, Maria, Virginia, and Peter—and Edgar pops out halfway and waves. Thrilled, the regulars pull Lacy into their company and gather around Edgar's grave. Maria—his Muddy—crouches down and plants a kiss on the top of his head. Loving the attention, Edgar improvises a new verse for his famous "The Bells" poem in a hushed whisper, and the residents, including Lacy, get into the rhythm, tapping their toes, nodding their heads, and eventually breaking into an absurd kind of tiptoe dance.

EDGAR *(singing)*:

Hear the shrieking of the bells
Midnight bells!
What a cheeky sneaky plan their creaking now foretells
While the moon is looking down
With a promise so complicit
Let us wake and start the ruse
with a gusto most illicit—
Feel the strong thrilling rush
Wink, wink, hush, hush
Let the longing for adventure ring out from the place
it dwells
With the bells, bells, bells, bells, bells, bells, bells,
Oh the reeling and the pealing of the bells!

Lacy can't help laughing. They are like kids at Christmas. Now, she decides, she will tell everyone that Sam is staying and that is that. But Mrs. Steele's door opens, and everyone jumps into their preplanned positions.

Edgar ducks back into his grave. Sarah quickly produces the teapot and the residents sit where they usually do, as if this were just another typical night. Billy is the only newcomer and he chooses to lean rakishly against Lacy's bench. Knowing that Mrs. Steele will expect her to be sitting on her bench, Lacy sits down next to Billy, tucking the undelivered note for Sam into her pocket.

As agreed, Peter and Dr. Hosler take their places in the shadows behind the church and wait until it's time for them to appear, and the rest gather as if for tea.

They all ad-lib small talk, pretending not to see Mrs. Steele.

MARIA *(to the Spindly sisters)*: Did you sleep well?
EFFIE and NEFFIE *(simultaneously)*: Quite.
MARIA: Perhaps Dr. Hosler was right, and our measured perambulation before daybreak induced slumber. I slept like the proverbial baby myself.

Maria holds her teacup out to Sarah, who pours, trying to hide the fact that her hand is shaking.

MRS. STEELE: You're all up early.
MARIA *(turns and acts surprised to see her)*: Come join us, Mrs. Steele. Nothing like a cup of tea.

Mrs. Steele sits at her usual place, and all watch rather nervously as Sarah sets out a cup for her. Just as she is about to pour, Sam rises.

He is on edge, as you can well imagine, assuming Lacy has read his bold declaration of love. He sees Lacy and Billy together and his heart wobbles. Although terrified, he forces himself to look at her, hoping she'll return his gaze with a glimmer of love for him in her eyes.

Lacy, thinking that what Sam needs right now is protection from any kind of attention from her, does not return his gaze. Sam quickly looks away, his heart breaking.

Mrs. Steele picks up her teacup, looking at the residents with distrust.

MRS. STEELE: Late to bed, early to rise . . . that is not typical Westminster behavior.

Anxiously Maria coughs to get Dr. Hosler's attention and give him a look that says: Let's move!

It's all going too fast, Lacy thinks. She had wanted to slip Sam the note before Mrs. Steele emerged. Now she doesn't know how she can give him the message.

Maria coughs again and Dr. Hosler nudges Peter, who comes forth ringing his bell, with Dr. Hosler at his side.

PETER: Oyez! Oyez!
MRS. STEELE *(turns abruptly to face them)*: What's this?
PETER: Hear ye! Hear ye! The President of the Committee for Safety and Tranquility has an announcement to make.

Peter turns to Dr. Hosler.

DR. HOSLER *(removing his hat)*: Good evening, all. On behalf of the Committee for Safety and Tranquility, I would like to introduce a new tradition of honoring a committee president who has shown outstanding leadership in promoting safety and tranquility with an Exemplary Service Award.
MRS. STEELE *(scowling)*: Whoever heard of such a—
DR. HOSLER: And the first recipient of the Exemplary Service Award will be Gertrude Steele, President of the Etiquette Committee.

A surprised smile alights on Mrs. Steele's face.

MRS. STEELE: Oh! Well . . . I suppose a new tradition can be started.

DR. HOSLER: It has been a challenging year and our stalwart Mrs. Steele has provided excellent leadership, which has, in turn, helped to secure the safety and tranquility of the good residents of Westminster Cemetery.

There is a round of applause, which Mrs. Steele very much enjoys.

Sam grows more despondent. Lacy's ruse—which is becoming more apparent to him now—is continuing without any interruption from Lacy to include him. Forget the idea of love, she doesn't even trust him, he thinks.

MARIA: Congratulations, Mrs. Steele. There is none more deserving.

EFFIE: Yes, dear.

NEFFIE: Quite right.

DR. HOSLER: The commendation will be given tonight in the subchamber of the catacombs where the declaration will be recorded for the Official Archives. A detail-filled and lengthy speech will be given to the honoree by myself, and we hope that a similarly exhaustive speech will be given by the recipient, which will also be written down word for word so that it can be published and read at any time by all.

MRS. STEELE: Speeches! Oh, this is a surprise.

MARIA: Do make it a long one, Mrs. Steele. Short speeches are so amateurish, don't you agree?

MRS. STEELE: Yes. Yes.

MARIA: Oh, I must say I'm envious! How I would love to be in your shoes, Mrs. Steele. But I daresay I don't deserve the accolades as you do.

Maria's lines are delivered with such cloying sweetness, we are sure that all will be ruined; but the inclination to believe what one wants to believe trumps bad acting. Mrs. Steele does not see through her. She merely nods and rises in a fog of pleasure.

DR. HOSLER: As kin, Samuel Henry Steele is also invited to be present.

Feeling the sting, Sam turns the color of ash. The irony! The invitation is an exclusion! Quickly he busies himself. Noticing his satchel on the ground, he hoists the strap over his shoulder.

Lacy says nothing, determined to slip him the note as soon as she has the chance.

As various residents step forward to congratulate Mrs. Steele, Lacy finds her moment. She brushes past Sam and drops the note in the side pocket of his satchel.

Dr. Hosler takes Mrs. Steele's arm and as they head toward the catacomb entrance, the residents form a line to wave and cheer them as they go.

[We are breathing a sigh of relief, aren't we, dear Reader? Sam will read the letter and all will be put to right. But it's too soon. For there is Billy edging his way to the door. Watch. Just as Sam passes by, he surreptitiously plucks Lacy's note out

of Sam's satchel and slips it into his own pocket. His own pocket! It's appalling. It's vile. It's enough to make one's blood boil. And none but us sees it.]

MARIA: Have a grand time!
BILLY: Congratulations, Mrs. Steele!
EFFIE: See you in a few hours.
NEFFIE: Take your time. Ta-ta!

Just as Mrs. Steele is about to go through the catacomb portal, she pauses. A lengthy sojourn in the catacombs will mean that she will likely miss an opportunity to give Lacy Brink her third strike. But I deserve this award, she tells herself. Dealing with the girl can wait a little longer.

MRS. STEELE *(to Sam and Dr. Hosler)*: Off we go.

Unable to look at anyone and not knowing what else to do, Sam follows his mother, diving through the doorway. Dr. Hosler, bringing up the rear, turns, winks at the residents, and shuts the door.

And since our attention cannot be in two places at once, we must leave Sam in his grief and embarrassment and Mrs. Steele in her excitement and Dr. Hosler in his dutiful determination, and focus on Lacy and her comrades in complicity, for as soon as the catacomb entrance closes, everyone leaps into action.

Maria and Owen both rush to Edgar and Clarissa's graves respectively to tell them that the coast is clear. Edgar hops out and gives his beloved Muddy and Virginia hugs and kisses. Clarissa rushes into Owen's arms.

Convinced that Sam will find her letter and make up some excuse to return, Lacy gives her full attention to the task at hand.

LACY: Okay! Let's get things in place quickly. We don't have writing time so this will be lots of improv, but take, like, at least five or ten minutes now to play around with what you have to say. I really want to encourage everybody to step up to the mic. Billy, can I rehearse a little with you? I need that beat again.

The hum grows. While Lacy and Billy rehearse, Sarah prepares tea, Maria tries to talk Virginia into performing, and Effie and Neffie set out the shawls and the centerpiece bouquets. Meanwhile Peter rushes to the graves of the brave souls who had attended the first open mic, whispering the news and encouraging them to come out. From George Babbitt, he borrows the cane and recreates the microphone.

After a few minutes, Maria, anxious that time will slip away, nudges Lacy to begin the show. Lacy takes her place on the stage and asks Peter to ring his bell.

All eyes are on Lacy. Excited and terrified, Lacy looks for Sam, in need of moral support. He still hasn't arrived. In the awkward silence, Billy jumps onstage and puts his arm around Lacy, a daring physical move that results in tittering from the audience.

BILLY *(into the mic)*: Ladies and gentlemen, please welcome Miss Lacy Brink.

More applause. Billy smiles and steps out of the way. Lacy thanks him and looks out at the audience. Seated on tombstone clusters around the stage are the regulars along with more than a dozen Sleepers. In clothes from various centuries and decades, they look as if they're models from a historical costume catalog. Emanating from them is a current of hushed intrigue, but underneath them all hums an even greater energy: the Suppressed and the other underground Sleepers are straining to hear what's going on.

LACY: Good evening! My name is Lacy Brink, and I have something to say, first to all of you who are pretending to be asleep right now. I'm sure some of you know who I am because you've been listening. I'm a Modern. And I'm President of the Entertainment Committee. And Mrs. Steele isn't exactly fond of me.

This understatement gets a laugh.

LACY: The first thing you should know is that Mrs. Steele isn't here. We gave her a prestigious award . . .

More laughs from those in on the joke. The souls below the surface begin to stir.

LACY: . . . and she is busy receiving it in the catacombs. Tonight we're going to do something different. We're going to have another open mic, but this one will be real. If you are afraid or if you disagree with us for trying, that's fine. All we ask is that you go back to sleep, mind your own business, and let us have this one night. If you want to join us, you are welcome. But first I'd like to introduce a new friend. Owen Hapliss, please come forward.

Instinctively, the residents stiffen as Owen walks up to the stage with his huge frame and heavy footsteps. Clarissa watches from the rear. Apologetically, Owen stops and looks to Lacy, but she beckons him forward and then speaks to everyone again.

LACY: Owen Hapliss is off duty. That means he gets to sit and enjoy the show.

Lacy smiles and waves at Clarissa to join him at a "table" near the front. Beaming but shy, she does.

LACY: Since Owen has the night off, that means anybody who happens to be Suppressed is welcome to come on out and join us. *(She pauses to let this sink in.)* I'm talking to you now, Suppressed people. You can come out. I know this is radical. You don't have to, of course, if you're scared. But if you want to come, you are welcome.

The door to the Watson crypt swings open. Hand in hand, Alfred and Agnes step out. They are that kind of couple that have come to look alike over the years, both a bit on the dusty side. Effie and Neffie rush to greet them. One by one, others join, Sleepers and Suppressed residents alike, and a hushed and giddy reunion begins. Clarissa's mother, father, and sister—Sleepers all—venture out and hug her tearfully.

Peter runs around to inform the residents buried on the

other side of the church. Cumberland peeks out and, seeing so many others, decides to step out. After a few minutes, a sizable crowd has gathered. There are still many who are afraid to come, but fifty of the 131 Suppressed souls have risen and seven more of the Sleepers. The little stage area is standing room only now, and the younger residents are climbing on the crypt roofs to get a better view.

Lacy continues.

LACY: All right, people. Welcome to the second Open Mic Night at Westminster Cemetery!

She pumps her fist in the air as everyone applauds. Again, she looks for Sam and is disappointed not to see him, but she can't slow down or let her energy falter. She has to do her job.

LACY: In case you hadn't noticed, we have a special guest here tonight, and I thought he could kick things off for us.

Lacy leans over and asks Edgar in a whisper if he is ready. Edgar nods.

LACY: Everybody, put your hands together for the one, the only Edgar Allan Poe.

SCENE 5: THE OPEN MIC

Edgar walks to the mic and all applaud. He turns and looks out at the audience, tears springing to his dark eyes.

EDGAR *(putting one hand over his heart)*: What a balm to my soul to know that you remember me. Thank you, dear friends and fans. *(Almost choking with emotion, he gathers himself.)* I shall now recite—

RAVEN *(puts one wing to his beak and calls out, masking his voice to sound like an audience member)*: Raven! Raven! Raven!

ALL: Raven! Raven! Raven!

The chant grows louder. One can only hope that Dr. Hosler is bringing Mrs. Steele to a place deep enough that she cannot hear the crowd's enthusiasm. Edgar smiles and raises his hand, and a hush descends.

EDGAR: I'm gratified that you want to hear my poem. In its day, "The Raven" was quite a sensation. But Lacy Brink has inspired me to perform something new.

A sudden doubt grips Edgar. His throat constricts. He has trouble drawing a breath. His pale face turns even whiter.

EDGAR: In truth, I may need another minute before I'm ready. This is harder than it looks.

Lacy steps forward. The humble honesty in Edgar's face is endearing. She feels as if she is seeing the real Edgar Allan Poe, not the frozen portrait on a book cover but an ordinary person who struggles, just like her, just like anyone else with writer's block. She decides to follow her impulse and gives him a hug, which he receives with awkward surprise.

LACY *(to audience)*: See, even Edgar Allan Poe gets nervous. It's natural. It doesn't mean that you're not good. It just means that you're human.

All laugh warmly. The atmosphere is gratifying, so different than when Mrs. Steele was present. Edgar smiles and whispers to Lacy to "kick things off." She nods and smiles. She's nervous, too. She closes her eyes and gets a beat going in her head and then her body rocks. She opens her eyes and nods at Billy to follow her lead.

Billy is standing on the side of the makeshift stage, and her trusting friendliness sends a hot ripple of shame through him. He knows that if she ever discovers his treachery, his chances with her are over. But his desire to enjoy the night, to once again feel the thrill of performing, pushes away the shame. He replicates the beat she's making with her body, one foot tapping out a rhythm on the stage, one hand adding syncopation with his stick on the roof of a crypt.

Lacy responds with an affirming nod. She gives herself a few more seconds to get into it, telling herself to focus, and then the words tumble out.

LACY:

Focus on the rhythm.
It's a given that you're gonna be nervous.
Just serve this up, spit it out, you can talk.
It's about letting go, it's not about the show.
So no telling lies. No wasting time.
No selling lines. No fake rhymes.
It's all about revealing when you step up to the mic.
Let out your feelings, you've got the right.

I'll 'fess up. I'm scared for real.
I'm a mess. Don't tell me death's no big deal.
I'm pissed at my murderer, pissed at the world.

(She picks up the scroll that Sam has left on the stone bench.)
Pissed at these rules. Wish they'd stay curled
in this goddamn scroll. We should bury it or tear it,
Send it to hell in a fucking chariot.

Lacy throws the scroll down, thrilled to let out some of these pent-up frustrations.

The crowd is shocked by her directness, and a handful of Sleepers quickly race back to their graves, too frightened to witness what they think will be mass Suppression. But the majority of residents are entranced by Lacy's opening. Her energy is infectious.

LACY:

We're supposed to be restrained, composed, contained.
If a lot tumbles out, people can't abide the pain.
They sing: "Hush, little baby. Don't you cry.

Hush and keep those eyes dry."
They build up a dam wall, a locked-tight door.
But now we're here, letting truth pour.
We're grabbing the moment. I feel like we stole it.
You need a white lie sometimes to reach your goal.
We're not hurting a soul. We're just giving each other
a little something to hold. So . . .
This is your story. Turn a new page.
This is your mic. This is your stage.

The rhythm continues. Lacy feels alive. Billy is ecstatic, too. Every molecule of his being has been longing to create this flow, an extension of his heart and body. He has been quiet for too long.

The driving beat and the fluidity of Lacy's words are gripping Edgar like a fever. He is longing to jump up and let a torrent of his own words out, but he pauses, caught up in the performer's worst impulse: he is thinking too much, trying to calculate what he could say that would be impressive.

It is Owen who walks up to the stage in two quick strides. He stands and faces the audience with determined sincerity. He has never done anything like this. He doesn't know if it is even possible, but there is something inside him that has to come out.

OWEN:

Wake up every morning,
shovel coal in the forge,
pump the bellows,
got to keep the fire stoked.

From the furnace to the anvil,
hammer and beat,
pull and twist,
pound and knead.

At least the iron beneath me couldn't feel.

I worked hard in life.
Couldn't stop for a breath.
But it was nothing compared
to what I have to do in death.

This job is my hell.
It's been like a cage
forcing me into
a monster I hate.

You're all afraid of every step I take.

He turns and looks out at Clarissa. She is sitting in her simple dress with the girlish bow, giving him her whole attention.

OWEN:

Then something came
to smooth the rough.
A smile from you.
That was enough
to get me through
the long, long days.

You went out of your way
to see me, to greet me.
I couldn't believe
that you bothered to care.
But I'd rise and
you were there.
I learned from you
what kindness can do.

I had no mother, no father,
no teacher but the smith
whose lessons were whipped
into my back.
Don't do this. Don't do that.
Don't expect a damn thing
but sweat and smoke and ash.

But that can't be all there is.
I know it isn't true
Because there's you.

Owen beams. He looks out at Clarissa, who rises and rushes to the stage as the audience claps. Her young round face is full of emotion. She is so happy to be receiving this love from Owen—and in public. But there is something on her mind. She speaks.

CLARISSA: I'm not an angel, not at all. I've had this weight on my chest . . .

(She gathers herself and steps up to the mic and sings.)

I had a group of friends, if you can call them that.
I never quite fit in although I tried.
I looked up to them. I don't know why.
They seemed to rule the world.
They seemed to hold the key.
I wanted them to notice me.

I was awkward but I wasn't the worst.
There was a pecking order from last to first.
A boy named Stephen, the smallest and skinniest,
was always the brunt of jokes.
I needled him to keep him in place.
I told myself he'd do the same.

One December day on our way home from school
we stopped at the pond by the old Price house.
It was cold. The pond had a layer of ice.
All those friends were there.
They were playing a game called Bet or Beware.
They needed someone to make up a dare.
I stepped up to look big in their eyes.
I told Stephen he had to walk on the ice.

As soon as I said it, I knew it was wrong.
But I started chanting and they went along.
I pushed him out. He tried to resist.
We all laughed as he fell and slid.
And I felt like a queen, like I had real power.
Then they pushed me out too.
A betrayal. A foul move
to prove that I could never rise above

my place.
I can still hear their laughter.
A slap in the face.

The ice groaned. Then I felt the crack.
I had already fallen onto my back,
and I remember how pretty the blue sky seemed
as I felt the ice shift apart beneath me.

Stephen went first; I could see him go.
Then the blue sky closed its eyes, and I sank below.

(Turns to Owen, ashamed.)
Now you know.
If I could do it again
I'd wake every day,
make it my goal
to be the one
to lift up someone else's soul.

Clarissa finishes and takes a breath. Owen takes her in his arms and she starts to cry. Even though it was hard to confess all that, Lacy can tell Clarissa feels better. The audience responds with sympathy. Together Owen and Clarissa return to sit together in the audience.

From way in the back of the cemetery, a Sleeper rises. It is old Gabriel Barr who was buried with his tin whistle. Inspired, he walks forward, finally playing a tune that has been haunting him ever since he died. The melody lifts them all and makes them want to cry.

SCENE 6: SAM BELOW

It has been at least seventy-five years since Sam has been in the catacombs. When his mother first died, he often descended into the church's moldy bowels to get away from her, making the excuse that he needed the quiet to memorize the rules for his job, although he disliked the atmosphere. The souls buried there, the original wealthy patrons of the church, were blue-blooded snobs who refused to mingle with the "Dirt Folk"—their name for those buried in the yard. Nine in total, the patrons tended to congregate in the main cellar chamber, gossiping and bickering. The exception was Hiram Chesterton, who preferred sleeping and yet had the habit of sleepwalking. Sam often sat in the passageway between the large and small rooms; and many a time, the sudden appearance of the old man walking toward him, staring at him with unseeing eyes, made the ethereal ether in Sam's veins run cold.

After a few decades, the catacombs became too depressing, and he opted to remain in the cemetery, where he would crawl on top of the Watson crypt and block out his mother's voice.

Now, as Sam walks down the crumbling steps toward the main crypt room, following Dr. Hosler and his mother,

he is sure he is sinking to the lowest point of his afterlife. The pale, bitter biddies and codgers who look up with surprise at their arrival make him feel worse.

DR. HOSLER: Ladies and gentlemen, I'm sure you know Gertrude Parsons Steele. She has been chosen as the recipient of the first annual Exemplary Service Award.

Standing between the doctor and Sam, Mrs. Steele puffs up like a peacock. The patrons are aflutter, whispering their surprise to each other, looking as faded and flat as a collection of old paper dolls.

DR. HOSLER: We are descending to the subchamber for the ceremony. You are welcome to join us.

The subchamber was chosen, Sam guesses, because it will provide the most insulation from aboveground noise. As they continue spiraling downward, now with the others tottering along, the sadness in Sam curdles into anger. Over the decades, he has tried to prove that his beliefs don't align with his mother's. He has had nothing but kind words for Virginia, Sarah, Maria, the Spindley sisters, and even Cumberland Poltroon. True, he never offered outright friendship to Owen, but he never mocked him or said anything unkind to him. As for Billy—well, Sam couldn't be expected to befriend every soul. Yet despite the years of effort on his part, the entire company is now rejecting him, deeming him to be untrustworthy.

Perhaps he should confirm their worst suspicions: wait until the bacchanalia above has most likely begun and then pull back the proverbial curtain for Mrs. Steele to see.

They reach the deepest chamber, Dr. Hosler talking loudly the whole way to mask any noise from above, when Sam is seized by the impulse to go back alone. He makes a pretense of searching through his satchel, then he turns to Dr. Hosler and his mother and whispers.

SAM: I must have dropped my pencil in the passage. I'll go fetch it and be right back.

He is gone before the doctor or his mother can protest.

Something in the boy's manner sets Dr. Hosler on edge. Sam has always been a sensitive young man, and perhaps their exclusion of him was a mistake, Dr. Hosler thinks. But the assembled group is waiting. Dr. Hosler cannot afford to deal with Sam.

For his part, Sam races up through the catacombs, heart pounding.

[If you recall, dear Reader, we left the open mic when old Gabriel Barr, the tin whistler, was playing his heart out. I must take a few moments now to catch you up.

While we were in the catacombs with Sam, Billy was moved to go onstage next. A better drummer than poet, he still delivered a surprisingly moving piece about his regret in never telling his mother how much he loved her.

Effie and Neffie followed with a humorous song about how much they enjoy their friendship even though they have had "a million tiffs."]

Now, as Sam readies himself to step out of the catacomb portal, Effie and Neffie are exuberantly singing their final chorus. It is an upbeat, catchy refrain, and Lacy sees the potential for audience participation.

LACY: One more time!

Lacy joins the two old women onstage to lead the audience in singing, and Billy jumps in to make a foursome.

[Dear Reader, I do not know if you have ever been in the situation of looking upon a party to which you were not invited. While there are more serious tribulations one can endure—tongue splinters, bayonet piercings, locust infestations, to name a few—gazing upon a sea of smiling revelers whose smiles are not meant for your eyes and hearing the strains of a melody that is not meant for your ears will induce a wave of self-pity that is undeniably agonizing.]

Here is what our poor Sam is faced with when he opens the door and peers out: Billy and Lacy onstage singing together. Of course, Effie and Neffie are there, too, but Sam doesn't notice them. Sam sees his beloved with his rival celebrating *la joie de vivre* . . . or rather *la joie d'après vivre*. The point is *la joie*. That is the picture Sam sees when he opens the door. Heartbreaking.

SCENE 7: THE OPEN MIC CONTINUES

At this point, we know what Sam does not: if he were to step out of his hiding place and declare his feelings for Lacy, she would stop everything and welcome him into her heart. Such an easy step when one knows the outcome, but the problem with life is that we have to live it without the benefit of a single crystal ball. Without knowing the certainty of the future, a simple action, such as opening a door, takes courage, and courage is what goes running back into the farthest corner when your confidence is low. And so Sam stays in the dark, his hand on the door, wanting to turn away but unable to stop watching.

Lacy is missing Sam and perplexed by his absence. She'd like to find him, but the spotlight is on her, and things are going far better than she expected, and so the show goes on. Effie and Neffie finish their song and Lacy steps to the mic.

LACY: Thank you! Let's hear it again for the Spindley sisters.

While the audience applauds, and Effie and Neffie return to their seats in the audience, Lacy looks at Edgar to see if he wants to be next.

Edgar is leaning against the Watson crypt, running his fingers nervously through his hair. He has been trying to decide what to perform and keeps changing the topic.

Awkward silence.

Lacy knows someone out there wants to get up, but no one is moving at the moment, so she takes the mic, signaling to Billy to get another beat going.

LACY:

From your seat to this stage might seem like a journey
that's too hard and risky to take.
But I know you're all tired of keeping it in.
You've been walking in silence day after day.
We can't let archaic authorities win.
Let's say what we need to say.

Who made the rules? Who made the ruler?
This afterlife state couldn't be crueler.
Who crafted this trap? Who does it serve and
who gives her the strikes? You know she deserves them.

She gestures toward Mrs. Steele's tombstone and the crowd reacts. They are growing rowdier. Raven, unable to contain himself any longer, flies to the stage, landing on the faux Greek head of a nearby statue, and engages in a series of rhythmic vocalizations that are known today as "beatboxing." The crowd loves it. Over the layered rhythms, Lacy keeps going.

LACY:

The Golden Rule I could live with, remember?

Just do unto others, yeah, watch your temper.
But why can't you scream when you need to scream?
Hell, we should be pissed if we're stuck and can't leave.

The Watsons and Smythes stand and cheer. Lacy smiles and continues.

LACY:

My rules would be simple and fair. Don't judge
the way I look. News flash: I don't care
who you think I should be.

Strike one if you're judging based on assumptions.
Society built on old views doesn't function
the way that it should, with kindness and love.

Sarah stands and applauds.

LACY:

Strike two if you slam me straight in the face
with an insult. Bad manners. That hater crap sucks.
Can't say something nice? Then shut the fuck up.

Effie and Neffie cover their ears, but they are giggling and nodding their heads to the rhythm. Agnes Watson stands again and shouts, "Amen."

LACY:

Strike three if you spend your time searching for sin
in your neighbors instead of looking within
yourself 'cause you're not immune to faults.

How about actively wanting to see us all
fall? That's called being malicious.
If that's not a sin, I don't know what is.

So let me shout. Let me scream. Let me blaze. Let me
steam.
Let me cry. Let me fall. Love will burn through it all.
Let me face my fear and rage. All the demons in the dark.
Let me sing with my soul and my strangely still-beating
heart.

The hum of energy from Lacy and the crowd is pulsing. Lacy is experiencing a high that she never thought possible. She looks out, wanting to share it with Sam.

From his hiding place, Sam watches in awe. He hasn't ever seen anything like it. He is more in love with Lacy and more despondent than ever.

Edgar, too, is struck—not with romantic love for Lacy—with the vivacity of the event. In his day, he was known for his performances full of carefully rehearsed drama; indeed, the ladies would swoon over him. But this is different, raw and authentic. He takes a tentative step toward the stage, but Sarah passes him with quick strides.

Lacy opens her arms to welcome Sarah onstage.

EFFIE *(calls out)*: Sarah! Oh my!
NEFFIE *(with gusto)*: Good luck! Very brave of you, dear!

Sarah smiles nervously and looks at Lacy, who gives her an encouraging nod. Sarah gathers herself and sings. Her voice is honest and lovely.

SARAH:

All my life I was told to be quiet:
Music and dance is the devil's riot.
Be a good girl and you'll be a good wife.
The key to salvation is hard work in silence.

Sarah smiles sympathetically at her husband, Peter. Peter nods at her. They have hardly spoken in all the years they have been at Westminster, not because of animosity but only because, although married, they were never close. Sarah continues, singing to Peter.

SARAH:

You carried me across the threshold line,
then it was you in your corner, me in mine.
We didn't know each other, strangers too young;
next thing we know a baby's coming.
And with it joy for the first time—oh—
a baby boy so sweet I could hold him
forever and breathe in the whole of him,
fold him inside my arms safe from the cold.

Three years later, he got sick and died.
I kept pressing my ear to his chest, trying
to hear his heart, to find a sign
that he could be alive; I couldn't leave his side.
The grief was like a tidal wave,
and all the people around me were praying and saying:
It's God's will. God must have wanted him.
You'll look weak if you weep and long for him.

Emotion pours out of Sarah. Peter sits on the edge of his seat, listening to his wife sing. He knew that she had suffered, but he is feeling as if he is truly seeing her for the first time.

SARAH:

Cook. Clean. Scour. Sweep.
Don't complain. Stay on your feet.
Iron, stitch, button up tight.
Cover up messes. Paint them white.
Put on your Sunday best. Say your prayers.
That ache in your chest? It isn't there.

Maria, Effie, and Neffie rise from the audience. Sarah has touched a chord that resonates for them. She repeats these lines and they sing with her in a round.

SARAH, MARIA, EFFIE, and NEFFIE:

Cook. Clean. Scour. Sweep.
Don't complain. Stay on your feet.
Iron, stitch, button up tight.
Cover up messes. Paint them white.
Put on your Sunday best. Say your prayers.
That ache in your chest? It isn't there.

SARAH *(singing alone)*:

I died in childbirth with my second son.
I never got to feel another one.
And the world went on without us, spinning,
And all this time I've been keeping it in.

Now I wish I would have told the world
to let me grieve, to let me feel my hurt.
Why did I always do as I was told?

Who says God loves being silent?
Aren't you tired of always lying?

Lacy joins Sarah and leads the refrain. Sarah sings, too, her catharsis huge.

SARAH and LACY:
Let me shout. Let me scream. Let me blaze. Let me steam.
Let me cry. Let me fall. Love will burn through it all.
Let me face my fear and rage. All the demons in the dark.
Let me sing with my soul and this strangely still-beating heart.

As Billy drums and Raven beatboxes and Gabriel Barr plays tin whistle, Lacy breaks out dancing. The crowd shouts encouragement, and Sarah begins to copy Lacy's dance moves. The crowd goes wild and the older women join in. As the women dance onstage, Sarah's release is so great that she is laughing and crying at the same time.

Sam closes his eyes. It is beautiful, and he isn't a part of it. He puts his face in his hands and rocks.

It's Peter who surprises everyone by rising next. Lacy and Sarah both encourage him to come up, and then the women return to their seats and Lacy steps back to give him center stage.

PETER *(terrified and determined at the same time)*:
I have never leaked this story before.
It's been buried deep under the core.
I've been wary of sharing it. It's been too scary
to think of opening the door and airing it.

(He looks at Sarah.)
All my life I felt different, which I hated,
I tried to fit in but I couldn't relate.
I had a boy's body but a girl's disposition.
I tried to control it but there were suspicions.

My parents are down there. Are you both listening?
Hoping I'll stay quiet. Truth is, wishing
the past didn't happen won't change that it did.
It's Pandora's box, and I'm lifting the lid.

When I was alone I would put on a dress
That belonged to my sister, her fanciest,
and I'd look in the mirror and see this face,
a girl inside, wanting to escape.

One day, my mother caught me and beat me.
She said, "Don't speak of this. Keep this a secret.
You know it's immoral and wicked. Defeat it.
Your father would kill you if he were to see it.
It's a sickness inside you, a virus, a cancer.
Quickly now, hide it. There's only one answer:
Deny this. It never happened and then
we won't speak of this ever again."

Am I wicked and immoral? Now that you know,
will you turn your back? Send me below?

Peter stops, shaking, close to tears. One of the Sleepers rises quickly and heads for the grave. Peter watches sadly. He takes a breath and turns.

PETER *(to Sarah)*:
We were neighbors. We married. I tried. You did, too.
It never seemed right. I know that you knew that
something was wrong. It wasn't you!
You were lovely and sweet and I wanted to please you,
but I felt like a stranger inside my own sleeves.

I loved our child, too, and mourned him in silence.
We sat at the table, said nothing about it.
I knew you were suffering and I had no clue
how to comfort or reach out to you.
I continued the pretense. Everything's fine.
But I wish I had tried. I wish I had said,
"Sarah, tell me your pain and
I'll listen and listen until you have said
all that you have to say."
That's what I wanted to give you.
That's what I needed, too.

Tears well in Sarah's eyes. Peter gathers strength. He has one more thing to confess.

PETER:
Am I wicked, immoral? I'll add to the list.

I died by my own hand, a knife to my wrist.

Billy stops drumming. Shocked silence. No one knew. Sarah stands up from her place on the side.

SARAH: Peter . . .

EFFIE *(whispering)*: This is consecrated ground, Peter. You shouldn't be here. I'm not saying that I agree with the rule, but—

NEFFIE: Anyone who takes his or her life is not allowed to be buried here. You're an illegal. If Mrs. Steele knew . . .

A woman rises from the Brown plot and rushes toward the group. Her hands are clasped to her chest, her face is drawn. She is the mother of Peter Brown. She stops a few feet from the stage and they look at each other deeply and compassionately, regardless of the fact that they have no privacy.

PETER: Mother.

MRS. BROWN: I wanted you here, so I lied. I was the one who found you, Peter. I couldn't bear the thought of you lying out there, somewheres. *(She points to the world beyond the gates of Westminster.)* And I couldn't believe that there'd be no mercy for your soul. *(Tears are streaming down her face.)* I told everyone you died by accident while you were cleaning fish. I didn't even tell your father. I took that secret to the grave. I didn't know what else to do. I never knowed what to do. I didn't understand any of it and still don't. I just tried to protect you.

Mrs. Brown stands, uncertain. Peter rushes over to her and hugs her. They both cry.

Sarah asks Lacy for her shawl, which has been around Lacy's waist, and fashions a dress with it for Peter. He cries harder and then smiles. They hug. As the three of them step back into the audience, the regulars rise and applaud.

Ecstatic, Lacy looks out in the hopes of seeing Sam. She cannot believe he is not here to share in this joyful release, and then the worry that something has happened to him begins to cloud her thoughts. She wonders about those catacombs and whether it's possible to get lost or stuck in them.

Virginia has been quiet so far, taking in everything. Now she stands.

VIRGINIA: I'll go next, Lacy.

Lacy nods. The audience hushes. Virginia begins singing as she walks to the stage. Her voice, forceful, comes from a place so deep in her, she had forgotten it was there.

VIRGINIA:

You all know me. I'll admit it:
Everything I long for is forbidden.
Don't get me wrong, I'm not into committing
major crimes or sins or Satan's bidding,
but I find that sitting or sleeping or keeping
my mouth closed, my hands composed,
my neck and ankles fully clothed and unexposed
makes me want to explode.

I want to laugh too loud and dance too long
and make love until inhibition is gone.
But all that is supposed to be wrong.

From her seat in the audience Maria stands, worried that her daughter has gone too far.

MARIA: Virginia, hush!

Virginia's flushed and expectant face falls. It had felt so good to finally speak the truth—and now here is the familiar silencing.

But Edgar steps over, places his hand gently on Maria's arm, and looks up at Virginia.

EDGAR: Keep going, Virginia.

Virginia smiles and gets back into the trance of the rhythm.

VIRGINIA:
I lie and pretend to be polite,
greet with a smile, all sweetness and light.
Meanwhile, I sneak out every night
of every week to seek a place where I can be
somewhat, sort of free.

Virginia glances at Cumberland Poltroon, and her glance reveals her lack of deep feeling toward him.

At this, an expression comes over Cumberland's face. In all the time he and Virginia have spent together, nothing of any depth passed between them. He suddenly sees life as a banquet, which he has made the mistake of looking at rather than eating. How stupid, he thinks. For a brief moment, he considers stepping forward to perform, but then he thinks of the effort and courage it would take to rise up, and his will to change shrinks. He tells himself that he doesn't need to see any more, and he slips back into the Poltroon crypt and goes to sleep.

Virginia sees him go and is not surprised. She turns back to the microphone and continues.

VIRGINIA:

I was pressured into matrimony—
just thirteen. How could I have known
what marriage would mean?
I was starving and freezing
while he was off writing.
I was growing up and
wanting more out of life,
wanting to be myself.
Not some porcelain wife on a shelf.

Virginia looks at Edgar, not knowing how he'll take it.

EDGAR: You didn't love me?

VIRGINIA *(face softening)*: I loved you, Eddy. I still do. But it wasn't easy being married to you.

EDGAR: I thought you were happy. I knew you didn't like being poor, but I thought you wanted to be Mrs. Poe.

VIRGINIA: I did, at first. But that changed. I remember waking up on my sixteenth birthday and feeling as if I were separate from my body. Who is *Mrs. Poe*? I thought. It *can't* be me. Later that day, I went to the market and a stranger—a boy my own age—smiled at me, and I was overcome with a feeling of desire that I had never felt for you. I had loved you, Eddy. I had admired you. But I had never felt that kind of desire for you. I didn't even know that it was lacking because I hadn't felt it at all until that moment. I'm sorry to say it, but it's true.

The audience is rapt. The open mic is veering away from performance, but Lacy recognizes the importance and does not interfere.

Edgar, somewhat embarrassed, feels compelled to defend himself.

EDGAR: Well . . . you know . . . many women found me exceedingly attractive.

Virginia smiles. Edgar is maddeningly adorable in his way. Something about that disheveled hair and those dark crooked eyebrows. He's a puppy, albeit a forty-year-old puppy, who just wants to be loved.

VIRGINIA: That's true, Eddy, but do you want to open the box of that topic? I can laugh about it now, but we both know that you carried on with women while we were married. I read your love letters to other women. I read their letters back.

EDGAR: Those were trifles. You were my true love. I worshipped you.

Virginia responds. Lacy had used that word to describe his love earlier. She was right.

VIRGINIA: That's the problem, Eddy. Worshipping is for statues. I worshipped you, too. You are a genius, after all. But you're also—you must admit—at least a tad deranged. Maybe we all are. Anyway, statues can't love and be loved. Statues aren't alive. I didn't feel alive in our marriage, but I didn't know how to acknowledge or express that. I became duplicitous and calculating and bitter and . . . *(she looks at Lacy, determined to go all the way)* frankly, a little jealous of anyone—particularly any woman—who seemed to have what I didn't have: an honest way of being in her own skin.

Lacy smiles at Virginia, and Virginia smiles back. Edgar takes in Virginia's words. He returns her honesty with honesty.

EDGAR: You have grown up. You're not my little wife anymore. I can see that, and I can see that I made mistakes. For that, I am truly sorry. I have always loved you and will always love you. Forgive me, please. You have my blessing, Virginia. Live your afterlife freely.

VIRGINIA: Thank you.

They embrace. No longer struggling to compose a clever poem, Edgar walks to the mic.

EDGAR:

I'm Poe. Yes, woe! I'm half deranged.
The beast inside is hard to tame.

So the drunk keeps drinking
though he wants to be sober.
And the lover keeps cheating
though insisting that it's over.
And the gambler who has quit
runs to place another bet
while his family tries to live on
cold soup and regret.

I'm employing the word "he"
But, of course, I mean me.
I apologize for my infidelities.
I professed true love but
was blind to your needs.

This impulse to hide
the truth is perverse.
I was my own worst enemy.
That's how it works.

We should shine the light
in the darkest of our places.
It's frightening and wild,
but that's where the grace is.

The audience applauds and Edgar smiles. Virginia gives him an affectionate pat on the back. Edgar turns and whispers, with equal affection.

EDGAR: Just so you know . . . being married to a thirteen-year-old girl wasn't easy, either.

Virginia laughs. Maria runs over and puts her arms around both of them.

Lacy looks out at the audience to see who will go next. She sees an older man walking toward the stage, a man who bears a resemblance to Sam, and her heart skips a beat.

From his hiding place, Sam also sees the man. Immediately he knows who he is, although they haven't met as adults. This is Sam's father. Jolted, Sam stands but doesn't move.

As the man walks tentatively to the stage and stands in front of the mic, Sam stares at him and Lacy stares at Sam.

[We need to take a moment to understand the intricacy of what is happening, dear Reader. Here is Henry Steele, a man who hasn't shown his face for over 160 years, and who looks terrified but resolute to finally step forward. And here is his son, our dear Sam, who is so shocked at the sight of his father that he has just revealed to Lacy the fact that he has been hiding behind a tombstone. And here is Lacy, who is simultaneously relieved that Sam is not lost or stuck in the catacombs and also worried about why he looks so distraught and yet also irritated at him for sitting behind that fucking tombstone for God knows how long when she had been missing him. While she would have been overjoyed to see him earlier, now her response is complicated. He has been at the open mic for how long, she wonders, crouching in . . . what, cowardice? . . . instead of offering support to her.]

HENRY STEELE *(a halting, rusty voice)*: My name . . . I'm . . . Henry Steele.

The audience is silent.

Henry stops and looks around, seeing Sam standing in the rear. The father's face lights up and then darkens with shame. He is frozen in the body of a thirty-five-year-old man: tall and muscular, crammed into the plain black, too-small suit, the one he got when he was married, the only one he ever owned, the one that the ladies at Westminster dressed him in for his funeral. He has a face like Sam's, only longer and stronger and harder, with a scar on one cheek. Light eyes and curly hair. Like Sam's. He stands holding one arm tightly against the side of his body with the other, as if he doesn't trust himself, with an astonished look on his face. Truly, he did not think his legs would lift him out of his grave and carry him here. He takes a breath and begins to speak.

HENRY STEELE: None of you know me. I died in 1852. Sam was four years old. After I woke up here, I went right back to sleep. Or at least I tried to sleep . . . I had a lot of time to think . . . and a lot of time to listen. I know what you all think of my wife. I know what you're doing right now.

There is a rustling in the audience as the residents look at one another uneasily. Henry continues.

HENRY STEELE: I worked for a bootmaker—I pegged the soles and the heels. Gertrude was one of the girls paid to sew the uppers. She was fifteen and poor like me and came once a week to get her new pieces and turn in the ones she had sewed. I fell for her and we married. But she was smart—too smart for me—and more ambitious. She had a knack for numbers and accounting and she read everything she could get her hands on. She wanted us to open our own shop, had all kinds of fancy ideas about shoes that were coming from Italy and France, but I didn't have that kind of head. We took a loan and had some bad luck and I started drinking.

Sam holds his breath. From the time Sam had first arrived at Westminster, he had been hoping his father would wake up. For decades he dreamed of talking with him, establishing a relationship. Now Sam feels the prickle of apprehension.

HENRY STEELE: That dark side he talked about . . . *(nodding at Edgar)* . . . I know all about that. I got deeper into debt and deeper into drink. It numbed me, but it also made me do things that I didn't want to do. I beat her and I beat those boys, my first two, Henry Jr. and Frank. They ran away. Broke her heart. I don't know what ever happened to them, whether they died young or lived long lives. They aren't buried here. *(Henry looks back at his own grave and then at the church.)* Every Sunday she went to this church and pretended that we were a good family and everything was fine. I didn't go. Somehow she must have scraped together money for our tombstones. It was important to her what people were to think about us. *(He looks back at Sam's grave.)* Sam came along. Spitting image of his brother Frank. Spitting image of me at that age. But he wasn't anything like me. Sam was like her. Smart as a whip, right from the start. She put everything into him. He started talking whole sentences practically before walking. He could do sums at the age of three, and he could read, too. So smart he kind of scared me. *(Henry's voice becomes thick.)* When I had a drink in me, he couldn't do anything right.

A queasy feeling takes hold of Sam's stomach.

HENRY STEELE: One night, Sam was scared to go to bed, and I wanted him to shut up, so I took him out back with a leather strap. He was like a little fawn, he was so small. Gertrude begged me to stop and I hit her harder than I ever had and told her to shut up.

An anguished sob breaks through Henry's tight throat. Sam starts to shake. Whatever irritation Lacy had toward Sam is overtaken by sympathy. She wants only to go to him, but she doesn't dare interrupt.

HENRY STEELE: I was going to kill him. She could tell. So she did what she had to do. As soon as I felt the blow on the back of my head, I knew. She has carried that secret . . . I know she is afraid that she will be judged, in the end, as a murderer, and so she has been trying hard to hide it, to make up for it by following the rules. *(He looks down.)* I know none of you likes her. I know you have reason. But . . . she . . . she has been trying to do the best she can. *(He looks out, baffled.)* As for me . . . I don't deserve to be here. I don't know why I'm here.

The crowd is silent.

To take down the scaffolding of a life that you thought was nailed into shape and replace it with new material is a herculean wrestle. Lacy and the residents begin the struggle to understand the woman they have thought of as their nemesis.

Sam tries, too, and for him it is the hardest. His father's confession makes him hate him, but he also admires his courage in finally coming forward, and those two opposing forces are colliding within his soul. He longs to rise and shout at his father, let him feel the raging whirlwind of emotions that he set in motion. But Sam does not move, and he hates himself for standing still.

Just when it seems the evening could not possibly grow more complex, Raven suddenly opens his wings and caws with alarm. He flies from his spot near the stage back up to his usual perch on the top of Poe's monument. Everyone freezes. There is a sound at the front of the cemetery. All turn to look. Olivia opens the gate.

SCENE 8: OLIVIA

Olivia enters.

The Dead are caught off guard, still reeling from the emotional outpouring, and now a living, breathing person has entered their domain. For the first few seconds they are silent, frozen, as Olivia walks toward them.

Lacy and Sarah and Sam know who she is. The others can see by Lacy's face that something important is about to happen.

Olivia has a bottle in her left hand—not even bothering to hide it—and her right hand is wrapped in a makeshift bandage. She's drunker than she's ever been and has begun to shiver. Half an hour ago she took a second painkiller too close to the first and washed it down with vodka that she sweet-talked an old man into buying for her. She has lost her coat—or rather Zane's—and can't recall the circumstances. The jeans and sweater she's wearing aren't warm enough.

As she walks among them, the Dead look at her and then at one another, not knowing what to do. Sarah quickly takes action. She moves through the crowd, whispering that Lacy will need time with her sister, that everyone should go back to their graves for the moment.

Lacy remains transfixed as the crowd disperses. The

core group—Sam, Sarah, Billy, Peter, Owen, Maria, the Spindly sisters, and Virginia—are too anxious about Lacy's well-being to leave her completely alone. They step back and stand still, not wanting to interfere, but wanting to support her. The two Suppressed souls in our group—Edgar and Clarissa—instinctively hide near their own graves, ready to dive under if Mrs. Steele should return.

Olivia faces Poe's monument and takes another drink. She glances up at Raven and then lifts her bottle to him. Lacy winces. The sight of the alcohol after hearing Henry Steele's confession is hard to bear. Lacy isn't prepared for this. It isn't fair for Olivia to be able to wander in whenever she wants.

Olivia's cell phone buzzes. She pulls it out and drops it into an empty flower urn with a laugh. Suddenly dizzy, she sits on Lacy's bench and closes her eyes. Lacy walks toward her sister.

LACY: Go home, Liv.

Olivia sets the bottle on the ground by her feet and begins rocking back and forth, rubbing her right arm with her good hand to warm it up. She has been holding her right hand up to stop the bleeding and her fingers have all gone numb.

OLIVIA: I wish we were little kids again, Lace.
LACY: You look terrible, Liv. Stop drinking. It's late. Go home.

Olivia tries to flex the muscles of her cold right hand but stops because it hurts.

OLIVIA: I slammed my fist into a mirror tonight because I couldn't stand the look of my own fucking face. *(A bitter laugh.)* Seriously. *(A long pause.)* I got fired tonight. Rob texted me. I don't blame him. I would fire me if I were him. I was supposed to show up tonight and I didn't. He said I probably needed time to get my head together and that maybe work wasn't a good idea. He was trying to be nice, but I got so pissed. I mean, really angry. I kept having this weird fantasy of smashing his face in mud. *(She shakes her head.)* I don't know what's wrong with me. I swear if he had told me he was giving me a raise I would have felt angry too.

Olivia takes another drink. Lacy tries to pull the bottle away although she knows she can't.

LACY: You're already drunk, Liv. Stop it.

OLIVIA: It's like Zane. No matter what Zane does, I get mad. I don't know if it's possible for one person to be this angry without something happening internally. I mean, I feel like my brain or my liver or my spleen or whatever the fuck is inside me is going to explode. I walk down the street and I have this fantasy of things exploding. The more he tries to help, the more he pisses me off. I'm even mad at you. Isn't that fucking ridiculous? I'm pissed at Mom, too, for going out that night, which is really fucked up because she deserves to have a life, and now she doesn't.

Olivia's words trigger a memory for Lacy. Once again, she is pulled back into a swirl of images from the night she died.

LACY: Don't say that. It's not Mom's fault, Liv. I remember. She told us about her date and we helped her get ready and told her to have fun. *(Lacy can see her mom's scared but excited face.)* I was afraid that if I had brought up the fact that I wanted to go out that night, she wouldn't have gone. So I didn't say anything until she had already left. Then I texted her and said that I was going out, but I lied. I didn't tell her that I wanted to go to the open mic. I told her that I had forgotten that I had a special chorus rehearsal. I thought she'd be so focused on her date that she wouldn't even answer and that I could just go. But she texted you. *(Another image floats in . . . the basement stairs.)* I'm remembering more. Diana and Zane and you and David were in the basement. And then you came up and yelled at me because Mom's text said you had to drive me to the school rehearsal and you didn't want to. We got in this huge fight . . . remember? We were standing in the kitchen.

OLIVIA: I read your poetry journal yesterday when I came home. God, Lace. Every inch of space in that notebook is covered with words . . . I mean, I knew you were into poetry. I just didn't want to take you seriously. That night in the kitchen, that night when I got that text from Mom to drive you—

Lacy is excited that Olivia is finally talking about that night. The memory comes . . . how Olivia looked that night, in the kitchen. She was wearing a black T-shirt and jeans.

LACY: Yes! We were in the kitchen!

OLIVIA: I was pissed at Mom for telling me to give you a ride to school, and I was pissed at you for needing a ride. You were standing there holding that poetry journal and you said to stop yelling because you were going to walk. Then you said I was too drunk anyway, and I got mad and pulled your arm and you dropped your journal and that flyer came out about the open mic at Tenuto's. I saw the date on it and it hit me that there was no school rehearsal. You wanted to go to the open mic. You had lied to Mom and you were lying to me.

A full memory comes to Lacy in a flash.

LACY: You were standing with your back to the sink. The light seemed so white. Really harsh. You picked up the flyer, and you asked me if that's where I was going, and I said yes. You were so mad, and I didn't understand why. I mean, I told you that you didn't have to drive me. I wanted to walk. You wouldn't let it go. You called me a liar and asked me why I didn't tell you about the open mic. For a second it looked like you were going to cry.

OLIVIA: When I saw that flyer it hit me that your poetry was probably really good, and that the whole evening at Tenuto's would be intense and amazing. We were standing there in the kitchen, and you had this expression on your face. You looked really sincere and really little to me, like the way you did when you were, like, seven. I had this moment where I could have been proud of you, but then this little flicker of hate ran through me, and I thought, "You think you're better than me. You're writing poetry, and I'm getting drunk with my friends. Well, fuck you." I asked you why you didn't tell me about it, and you gave me this look like I was an idiot for asking. You said, "You'd just ridicule me, Liv. Why would I tell you anything?" And so what do I do? I walk over to the basement door and yell down to my friends. I say, "My little sister wants to go to an open mic because she thinks she's got talent." Diana's laugh floated up from the basement. I hated myself, even as it was coming out of my mouth.

Lacy is silent. Olivia takes another drink.

OLIVIA: I did stuff like that to you all the time, Lacy. I was jealous. You were doing something positive. You were putting yourself out there. God . . . an open mic. You had guts.

LACY: I remember Diana's laugh. I got furious. I grabbed the flyer out of your hand and I told you that I was leaving and that I was going to text Mom to let her know that you were too drunk to drive me. Then you slapped me. I couldn't believe it. Right across the face. I can still feel the sting. *(Lacy puts her hand to her cheek.)* We both got quiet for a second. Then I turned and walked out. The last words I heard from you were, "Fuck you."

Olivia stands up, stumbles, and leans against a crypt for balance.

OLIVIA: Oh God. I'm going to be sick.

Now the memories are streaming into Lacy's mind. She looks off into the distance and recounts how the evening unfolded.

LACY: I remember everything . . . I wanted to walk. It felt good to be out in the air. It had rained and the streets were wet. I was nervous, but excited. All the way there, I went over and over the poem in my head and I kept checking my cell phone to make sure I wasn't going to be late. I had to wait at the intersection right across from Tenuto's. I was almost there. The door of the café was open and the light was pouring out. Voices were pouring out, too. I could hear people in Tenuto's all the way across the street, and I started to panic a little, realizing it was probably packed. I was waiting for the Walk sign and rehearsing the poem in my mind. And then I looked up and saw it with perfect clarity. The light was turning red and a blue pick-up truck gunned into the intersection just as a black car turned from the left. The black car didn't have its lights on for some reason. I noticed that. It all happened so fast, but I was noticing so much.

Olivia's eyes are closed. She is gripping her stomach. Lacy continues, almost in a trance.

LACY: The truck hit the car and, at first, I just thought about the guy in the car, because I could see him, and then the car spun and started rushing toward me. At first I had this false sense of security because I wasn't standing in the street, you know, I was standing on the sidewalk, pretty far from the curb. But then the car jumped the curb, and in that second before impact, I knew I was going to die. It was so strange. I could picture my body, so fragile. Against the coming force of all that metal I might as well have been made of sticks and paper, I thought. I was panicking but I was also calm and all these thoughts came to me. Really complicated thoughts. It must have only been a few seconds, but I was able to think. I thought about how the drivers of both the car and the truck were going too fast, and I thought about how sad it was that I was going to die this way because speeding through intersections was Mom's pet peeve. *(She looks at Olivia.)* Remember? Mom would slam her hands on the wheel if she saw someone run a red, and say, "Go ahead. Put everybody else in danger so you can get wherever you're going thirty seconds faster." And then she'd turn to us and say, "Girls, don't be like that."

Lacy continues, pacing. Sam's eyes are filling with tears. He is listening intently, sympathetically.

LACY: I'm remembering everything. It was like time stopped and all these thoughts were going through my head. While the car was spinning toward me, I was also thinking about the fact that if I hadn't waited on the sidewalk for the Walk sign, if I'd run across the street on the Don't Walk when I'd first arrived at the intersection, I'd be safe. The injustice of that struck me. We follow the rules, I thought, and we expect everyone else to do the same, and yet I'm going to die and the drivers who are breaking the rules will climb out of this alive.

The cold has gripped Olivia and she shivers. Lacy looks at her.

LACY: And at the same time, I was thinking about you, Liv. I was thinking about how screwed up it was that you were supposed to drive me to keep me safe, but how that wouldn't have been safe because you were drunk, and how ironic it was that I was going to end up dead anyway.

Sadness emanates from Lacy and the power of it causes the same hum to resonate from the Dead around her.

Olivia feels something in the air and drops her bottle. When she bends to pick it up, dizziness sets in. She tries to sit down and falls to the ground. The complexity of what she is carrying feels like a weight in her chest. She looks back at the ground where she and her mother buried Lacy's ashes and begins to cry.

Lacy watches her, trying to make sense of it all.

OLIVIA: You didn't tell on me, Lacy. I thought for sure you did. I thought you followed through with your threat and texted Mom about me being drunk and so I was just waiting for the ax to drop. And then my phone buzzed. It was Mom calling. It was—I don't know—maybe an hour and a half after you had left. I didn't answer. She called three more times and I didn't answer. I thought I was in trouble and I couldn't face it. And then the text came: "I'll be home in 15 minutes. Where are you?" I read it and I thought, Oh fuck. I made Zane and Diana and David leave. I made myself throw up and then I cleaned up the basement and drank a couple of glasses of water and ate a peanut butter sandwich and sat down at the dining room table with my homework, thinking I could bullshit my way out of it. Mom walked in the door and I was ready to deny the whole drunk thing, and then she sat down and started sobbing. Sobbing. It was terrifying. I didn't know what was going on. Her eyes were so wild. She finally managed to tell me that you had been killed, and it felt completely unreal. I was trying to understand it and then she told me that it happened on Crimmson Street. She said she didn't understand what you were doing there. She looked right at me with her red eyes and said, "You drove her to school, right?" In that moment,

I realized that you hadn't told her anything about me, and I felt this incredible relief because all I could think about was that I didn't want the blame. You're dead because of me and all I'm thinking about is how I won't be able to handle it if Mom is mad at me. *(Olivia drops her head and weeps.)* So I lied, Lacy. I told her that I drove you to school and dropped you off and that I had no idea how or why you went someplace else instead. You know how fucked up that is?

Something shifts in Olivia. In an angry burst, she stands and hurls her bottle against the church wall and screams. The intensity of it pulls her off balance. The world spins and she passes out, crumpling to the ground. Lacy rushes to her.

LACY: Liv!

Lacy's voice is too loud. It is late and she is too close to the catacomb entrance. Everyone but Lacy is aware of the danger.

Sam wants to pull her away, but Billy runs to her.

BILLY: Lacy—shh!

Lacy pushes him aside.

LACY: Get up, Liv! Get up!

The catacomb entrance opens. Everyone freezes. The two Suppressed souls who are still out—Edgar and Clarissa—only have time to duck behind tombstones for cover. Mrs. Steele hustles out, Dr. Hosler trailing after her.

MRS. STEELE: I heard you screaming, Lacy Brink. Strike three! You are now officially Suppressed!

A sickening, exhausted silence follows. Lacy feels as if the fog has returned, a thickness in the air that is making it seem difficult to breathe. She looks at Olivia, passed out, her hair covering her face.

LACY: But my sister . . .

MRS. STEELE *(follows Lacy's gaze)*: Your sister? Intoxicated . . . disheveled . . . reeking of alcohol . . . shameful! Two peas in a pod, I see. Well, she is not our concern, thank goodness. You are—

LACY: I have to help her.

MRS. STEELE: You are Suppressed. *(She looks out at everyone with a satisfied smirk.)* This whole ordeal is finally over!

Lacy puts her hand on a nearby crypt to steady herself. Trying to process her own fate and her sister's guilt and pain is too difficult. The stories of pain endured by Clarissa, Owen, Sarah, Peter, Virginia, Edgar, Sam, Henry, and, yes, Mrs. Steele are still ringing in her ears. Life seems impossibly complex. Her sister is tangled up in addiction and remorse, and there's nothing Lacy can do about it. What comes after death? More fear? More hiding from the truth? A sad, beaten look comes over Lacy's face. She says nothing.

SAM *(steps forward)*: Mother—

MRS. STEELE: To sleep, all of you.

SAM: Mother—

MRS. STEELE: Samuel! I said, to sleep.

LACY *(closes her eyes)*: She's right. Leave me alone, Sam. Go back to sleep—

SAM: No. This cannot stand. Mother—

LACY *(exhausted)*: Sam, don't get a strike for me.

SAM: But Lacy—

LACY: Sam, it's too late.

Billy puts his hand on Sam's shoulder. Now that Lacy is Suppressed, Billy's interest in her and his desire to thwart Sam are both moot.

BILLY: She's got the third strike, Sammy boy. We might as well go back to sleep.

The self-centered interruption from Billy has a wonderful effect on Sam. It shows him exactly how he does not want to behave. Sam turns to Billy and looks him square in the eyes with confidence.

SAM: Good night, Billy. Enjoy your sleep.

Clueless, Billy shrugs and picks up his drumsticks and walks off. Without a confession or apology, he simply takes his bad deeds with him to his grave.

[We, dear Reader, might even feel a little sorry for Billy at this point, for in choosing to be selfish, he has squandered the chance to expand his soul. But we will follow Sam's gracious lead and bid Billy adieu and turn our attention where it deserves to be.]

SAM *(turns to Lacy)*: I have been a coward, Lacy. I'm sorry it took me so long to come forward—

MRS. STEELE: Enough! Ever since this girl arrived, she has been—

Sam brushes past his mother, walks to Lacy, and looks at her tenderly.

SAM: Wonderful. Ever since you arrived you have been wonderful, Lacy.

MRS. STEELE: Stop it—

SAM *(ignoring his mother)*: You have this way of lighting up the dark, Lacy. My soul feels connected to you. I know we haven't known each other long and you might not feel the way I do, but I love you, Lacy. I don't expect you to say anything in return, but I want to say it out loud—

His words come to Lacy like colors in a dream. A knot of guilt rises in her throat. Nothing will change here, and all she has done is make it worse.

LACY: Don't, Sam. I screwed up. I put everybody at risk and—for what? Because I wanted to have an open mic? What good is opening up and expressing your emotions when all you get is more pain? When I first got here I thought the Sleepers were crazy for giving up, but now I think that's smart. It's too hard.

She walks toward her grave.

MRS. STEELE: Finally. A little reason. I, for one, am looking forward to the restoration of order.

Sam stands tall. His voice rings out.

SAM: Fuck the restoration of order.

Lacy stops.

Mrs. Steele looks at Sam. Her left eye is twitching imperceptibly. Her heart is racing. No one says a word. Then she turns her back to Sam and faces the group.

MRS. STEELE: It has been a long night. I suggest that everyone go to bed.

SAM *(anger rises)*: I know you heard what I said, Mother. Go ahead, give me my third strike.

Mrs. Steele steps close to Sam.

MRS. STEELE *(whispers)*: Don't do this, Samuel.

SAM *(steps back)*: Rules are funny, aren't they? People in power get to apply them—or not—as they see fit. People who aren't in power are at the mercy of the rulemakers and the rule upholders.

MRS. STEELE: You're talking nonsense! The rules are the only things that we can control. Basic decencies keep us civil—

SAM: Not if the rules themselves are flawed, Mother. Deep down, I think you know that. *(Gently)* You're flawed. I am, too. We're all flawed.

That left eye won't stop twitching. Mrs. Steele squeezes her eyes shut tight for a moment and then opens them again. Her son, standing before her, looks changed—older, but that's impossible.

MRS. STEELE: Samuel, how could you? I have tried all these years to protect you—

SAM: I didn't want that. How do you think it has felt for me to watch good people go under while I remained free? Do your duty, Mother. Give me my third strike.

A curious thing is happening inside Mrs. Steele. She feels as if the invisible internal stitches that hold her soul to her body are unraveling and her soul is falling down inside the shell of her body. She has a thought—*I am dying*—while simultaneously being aware of the ridiculousness of that thought. Her body is starched and standing while the rest of her is in a puddle. Words come out of her mouth, and she doesn't know how it is possible.

MRS. STEELE: Samuel Steele, that is strike three.

Lacy puts her face in her hands.

Mrs. Steele sways on her feet, thinking that she is like one of those chickens at the market that would walk around for a few seconds after its head had been chopped off.

Like the ghost he is, Henry Steele rises out of his grave, and a shudder runs through Mrs. Steele. With surprising tenderness, Henry goes to her and takes her hand.

HENRY: I'm sorry for everything, Gertrude. For how you had to live and what it did to you.

Anxious not to lose her composure, Mrs. Steele pulls her hand away. The last bit of starch that is holding up her body is evaporating. She tries desperately to stand tall.

MRS. STEELE: I do not know what you're talking about. *(She turns to Lacy and Sam, avoiding Sam's eyes.)* You have both been given strikes. According to Rule 231, the Suppression is immediate and— *(She turns to Owen.)* Owen Hapliss, do your job.

Everyone looks at Owen, who steps forward.

OWEN: I will not.

Now the world tilts and Mrs. Steele has to put her hand against the roof of the nearby crypt to catch her balance. Owen Hapliss has been firm ground on which she has been able to stand for more years than she can count.

Edgar, who has risen from his hiding place behind a tombstone, applauds.

MRS. STEELE *(turning to Edgar)*: Who are you?
EDGAR: Edgar Allan Poe.

Clarissa Smythe steps out from behind her tombstone and stands next to Owen. Mrs. Steele presses her other hand against her stomach.

MRS. STEELE: Owen Hapliss, strike three for refusing to do your duty. We clearly have souls here who need to be Suppressed. *(She turns to Maria, her voice growing weaker.)* Mrs. Clemm, I hereby proclaim that Owen Hapliss is relieved of his duties as Suppressor and that you appoint another in his place.

Another silence. Maria steps over to join Owen, putting a hand on his shoulder.

MARIA: I'm sorry, Gertrude. But no.

Mrs. Steele looks from resident to resident. She doesn't understand it. She has just sentenced her own son and the girl and Owen to Suppression. Instead of the hostile looks she was expecting from the others, they are gazing at her with a kind of soft sympathy. She doesn't know what to make of it. The entire experience is dizzying.

Lacy, too, feels dizzy. Sam's love is radiating toward her. She doesn't want to return to her grave, but she doesn't have the strength to fight. She sits on her bench, struggling for breath, as if she were trying to stay afloat in a deluge.

And then, like a lifeline, a voice comes from just outside the cemetery gate. Lacy knows it immediately. It is her mother's voice calling Olivia's name.

Lacy stands and looks.

LACY: Mom.

Deborah Brink is standing at the gate. She has left the house in a hurry, has thrown her coat over her pajamas and slipped on her black boots. Her eyes are red and her nose is running. Lacy always thought of her mom as solid and tough. Tonight she looks fragile and frightened, searching for sight of Olivia among the dark shapes of the tombstones and crypts.

In the shadows near the back, Olivia hears her mother's voice, too, and wakes.

The Dead do not move.

As Deborah pushes open the gate, Olivia doubles over and vomits. The mother hears something . . . she isn't sure what . . . and she calls again. Quickly Olivia wipes her mouth and slips into a shadowy hiding space between the church wall and a crypt. She clutches her stomach and shivers more violently.

Unable to see Olivia, Deborah walks in slowly, looks around, walks right past Lacy, and sits down on Lacy's stone bench.

She hasn't been back to the cemetery since that day, over a month ago, when they brought Lacy's ashes, a garden trowel, Lacy's poetry journal, and a bouquet of flowers. They had come in the early evening, when it was still light enough to see but after the street had quieted. They picked the spot by the bench because the space around the bench had no other graves. The dirt was firmer than she thought, but they dug a hole and buried the ashes quickly, knowing they didn't have permission. Deborah didn't like the secrecy, but she didn't know what else to do. She had looked at three other cemeteries, but they seemed like meaningless choices. After Olivia had mentioned that Lacy liked to write poems in this cemetery, Deborah had read Lacy's poetry journal. In between a poem about school and one about music, she found one about Westminster being her only place of peace. The day of the burial, Deborah had brought the journal, intending to read that poem from it, but the whole thing was too hard. She stood and cried with a swollen throat, feeling like a failure. Olivia couldn't speak either.

The flowers were, of course, gone now. The groundskeeper assumed they had come from Poe's grave—literature lovers sometimes left flowers at his grave—and he had raked them up the day after the burial.

Deborah had driven past the cemetery several times since then, but she couldn't stop. She felt guilty about driving on, but she couldn't face it.

Tonight she forced herself to come because she thought she'd find Olivia here. It was a hunch, but she was sure it was the right hunch.

Now she is staring at the place where her youngest daughter's ashes lie and wondering whether her oldest daughter is okay. One more time, she checks her cell phone, hoping to see a text from Olivia. Nothing.

She looks at the ground and tries to see Lacy in her mind. For some reason, the picture that comes to her is of Lacy and Olivia at the dinner table. It was maybe a week before Lacy died. They were teasing each other about who deserved the last piece of garlic bread. None of them had any idea what was to come.

She speaks, her voice barely a whisper.

DEBORAH BRINK: Lacy . . . sweetheart . . . what am I going to do?

LACY *(softly)*: She's here, Mom. It's okay. Olivia is here.

DEBORAH BRINK: If I lose both of you . . .

Deborah starts to cry, and tears well in Lacy's eyes. The Dead stand transfixed, silent.

DEBORAH BRINK: We miss you so much, Lacy.

LACY: I miss you, too.

DEBORAH BRINK: It's not fair.

LACY: No. It's not.

A sob comes out of Lacy. Hearing these words from her mother releases something in her. She feels as if the pain that was too big for her to hold is now outside of her, in a space that is big enough to contain it.

DEBORAH BRINK: I'm failing her. I failed you.
LACY: No, you didn't. It's not your fault.
DEBORAH BRINK: I got caught up in things. I didn't listen. I shouldn't have gone out that night—
LACY: Don't blame yourself. We can't make perfect decisions when we don't know what's going to happen.
DEBORAH BRINK: I've been sleepwalking through life, Lacy, ever since it happened. I go to work and get home and take a sleeping pill. I haven't been there for Olivia. I woke up tonight and she was gone. I don't even know where she is.

Deborah's tears flow. In the midst of her anxiety, she feels a sense of gratitude. She needed the push to come here. She needed to say all this.

LACY: It's not too late. It's going to be okay.

The exhaustion Lacy felt before is gone. Brimming with urgency, she runs to Olivia's hiding place.

LACY: Olivia, you have to come out and face this.
SARAH *(steps forward)*: They can't hear you.

Sam stops her. He knows that Lacy is responding instinctively. He'd do the same.

Lacy is too engrossed to notice. She is focusing on Olivia, who is sitting on the ground, her head back against the church, her eyes closed, shivering uncontrollably, trying to stay silent.

LACY: Liv . . . come out.

Deborah wipes her face and stands. Lacy panics.

LACY: No! Mom . . . don't go! Liv needs you. She's drinking too much. *(She turns to Olivia.)* Liv . . . you can't hide. You can't keep how you're feeling a secret.

Deborah bends down, kisses her fingertips, and presses them into the ground.

DEBORAH BRINK: I love you, Lacy.

Tears stream down Lacy's face. She watches helplessly as her mother starts to leave. Lacy turns back to Olivia.

LACY: Liv . . . don't you see? You need help.

Lacy looks at Sam and the souls she has come to know. They are standing among the gravestones, as helpless as she is. Their secrets, their regrets, the things about themselves that they wished they had faced in their lifetime seem to be swirling around them like a fog.

LACY: You can't be like us, Liv. Don't pretend that you're not in pain. Talk about how you're feeling and what happened. You have to ask for help because it's hurting you and what's hurting you hurts other people. You are chained down right now with all this regret and guilt, but hating yourself only makes it worse. You think that's the way you can pay me back for saying fuck you? It's not, Liv. I don't want that. Shine the light in the darkest part. I know it's hard. But if you don't do it, you won't be alive! This is your chance to be alive, Liv. You have to take it.

Olivia is shivering, gripping her knees, looking out through the space, watching her mother turn to go. Lacy crouches down in front of Olivia.

LACY: You think that what you're feeling now is going to be the way you feel tomorrow and the way you feel the next day and on and on, but the truth is you don't know what the future holds. There are good people out there, people you don't even know now who you will connect with. *(She looks at Sam.)* They'll make you smile and you'll make them smile. You don't even know them right now, but they are out there, Liv. And you think Mom won't forgive you, but she will. She needs your forgiveness as much as you need hers. She needs you, Liv, the real you.

Their mother turns back for one last look at the cemetery. Olivia, in her hiding place, sees her and catches her breath. For a moment, Lacy thinks Olivia is going to call out for her, but then Deborah turns. Without making a sound, Olivia starts to cry.

LACY: Say yes to it all, Liv. Do it for us. Do it for me. It's what I want. I love you, Liv. *(A funny sound comes out of Lacy, a half cry, half laugh.)* We're sisters. You've been remembering the times you hurt me, but we had fun, too. When we were little, we put on those plays, Liv. Remember? And then we saved up our money and went all by ourselves to secretly see *Cabaret* at the Hippodrome. We thought we were sophisticated. Remember? And that teasing song wasn't the only song you sang to me. Remember the no-sleeping song? At night, when I was scared to go to sleep, you used to sing me that song. You made it up for me. Remember? I loved it. I'd be there, smiling in the dark, singing along with you.

(Tears streaming down, Lacy sings brokenly.)
You don't want to go to sleep.
I don't want to either.
We don't want to close our eyes.
We don't want to say good-bye to the day.
So we're gonna sing a song.
Gonna sing it all night long.
Come on, sing it with me, Lacy.
Fa-lee la-lee la-lee lay.

Olivia doesn't move. Lacy looks toward the front. Their mother is opening the gate. Lacy doesn't know what to do. She turns back to Sam.

LACY: Help me, Sam.

Sam's eyes are glistening. He turns to Raven, perched on Poe's monument.

SAM *(to Raven)*: They'll hear you.

Raven lifts off and lands on Lacy's stone bench. In the quiet darkness, he trills the childhood melody that Lacy has just sung.

From her hiding place in the shadows, Olivia looks out, startled. Deborah stops at the gate and turns. For a moment, we see what they see: a black bird singing on a stone bench in an otherwise empty cemetery. The bird turns his head to look at Olivia, and a spark ignites inside of her. The bird sings again, and Olivia's heart seems to catch fire. Tears well in her eyes.

OLIVIA *(whispers)*: Lacy.

Olivia crawls out of the shadows and stands. Olivia can feel that Lacy is listening. This is her chance. She takes a deep breath and closes her eyes.

OLIVIA: I love you, Lacy.

The words come to Lacy like a kiss. Lacy cries.

LACY: I love you, too, Liv.

Sam steps to Lacy's side and holds her hand.

Raven lifts off the bench and flies back up to his usual perch, and the Dead step back.

Deborah runs into the cemetery and Olivia rushes into her arms. As they walk out together, Olivia begins to talk.

SCENE 9: THE RULES

The cemetery is quiet. Lacy and Sam are standing hand in hand, watching Olivia and her mother cross under the streetlamp and disappear into the darkness. Maria, Edgar, Owen, Clarissa, Virginia, the Spindly sisters, Peter, Sarah, and Dr. Hosler step forward. Mrs. Steele and Henry remain motionless.

LACY: Do you think they'll be okay?
SAM: Yes.
LACY *(turns to Sam)*: Thank you.

They hug.
Edgar speaks up.

EDGAR: What now?
CLARISSA: We can't go back to the way things were.

There is silence as this is contemplated.

SARAH: What about making new rules, as Lacy suggested in the open mic? Rules that make sense.
OWEN: No more Suppression.

SARAH: Be kind. Be tolerant.
VIRGINIA: Be honest.
SAM: Allow for grief and for the full expression of emotions.
MARIA: Comfort those who are in need of comfort.
EDGAR: Share power wisely.
EFFIE: Encourage music, poetry, dance, art, and the expression of feelings as a way of not only coping with death . . .
NEFFIE: . . . but also celebrating life!

Mrs. Steele steps forward. She is struggling to understand.

MRS. STEELE: But . . . the rules can't be changed.
LACY: Why not?
MRS. STEELE: They were given to us by the Authorities.
LACY: But who are the Authorities?

Everyone is silent. No one knows. Mrs. Steele tries to answer.

MRS. STEELE: They are the ones who came before us, who were appointed to the positions. They were . . .
LACY: . . . people like us? *(She looks at everyone.)* What if this whole system of rules was created by people so that this existence we're in has some kind of order? What if obeying these particular rules has nothing to do with whether or not you progress to whatever is beyond this place, if there is anything at all? What if what's beyond this place is so huge and beautiful and mysterious that no ordinary rules apply?
DR. HOSLER: None of us knows.

LACY: Exactly. What if the Authorities who made up the rules didn't know either?

MRS. STEELE: We need the rules to stay civilized. If there were no rules, we'd have a cemetery full of chaos. It's happening right now.

SAM: But this isn't chaos right now, Mother. This is civil dialogue. And look—Edgar and Clarissa and Lacy and Owen and I should be Suppressed according to the rules, but we're standing here and we haven't been struck by lightning.

VIRGINIA: I always suspected that the Authorities were just people like us.

Mrs. Steele walks over and sits on Lacy's bench. She is dumbfounded by how this is unfolding.

MRS. STEELE: I know you all hated me for being strict, but I didn't know how to do the job without being strict. How do you decide what's right and wrong? How do you hold the line? If someone breaks a rule, do you give a warning or a strike? When is a transgression normal and when is it dangerous? In one man's hands, alcohol is a warm friend; in another man's hands, alcohol is a demon. *(She looks at Henry.)* I decided early on that the safest path was to stick by the rules. I hated my job, but I did it because I thought it was necessary. I did it because . . . *(She looks at Sam, her face opening.)* I've been scared . . . I've been . . .

She stands up, not knowing how to put into words everything she is feeling. Effie steps forward helpfully.

EFFIE: You've been saddled with a lot of responsibility. I wouldn't have wanted your job.
NEFFIE: I would have gone quite insane.
EDGAR: We're all a tad deranged.
MRS. STEELE *(turns to Sam)*: I was trying to protect you.
SAM: I know.

Sam steps toward his mother, thinking that perhaps he should offer a hug, but she gives him a little nod of her head to show that, regardless of the recent upheavals, Gertrude Parsons Steele is still not the hugging type. Still, what passes between them is monumental. Sam returns to Lacy and squeezes her hand.

The sky is lightening almost imperceptibly, but Peter notices and reaches instinctively for the bell tucked in his belt.

PETER: It's almost sunrise. I should be making the rounds.

Everyone looks at the sky. Raven caws softly. A thought comes to Lacy.

LACY: If we don't have to follow the Suppression rule, what about the sunrise rule? What would happen to us if we didn't go back to our graves?

The question hangs in the air for a few seconds.

MARIA: Maybe nothing bad would happen to us.
VIRGINIA: You told me that if I let the sunlight touch me, I'd cease to exist.

MARIA: I didn't know for sure. I was afraid you wouldn't follow the rule.

SARAH: Maybe something wonderful would happen to us.

VIRGINIA: Maybe that's what it takes to progress. Maybe we'd go on to a better place.

PETER: Or a better state of being.

EDGAR: Something beautifully incomprehensible! Maybe we'd become vibrations of pure bliss in the vastness of infinity beyond the luminiferous ether.

EFFIE: That has a lovely sound.

NEFFIE: Quite.

Mrs. Steele stands, suddenly anxious.

MRS. STEELE: What if it's worse? What if it's nothing? Dust to dust.

SAM *(turns to his mother and smiles)*: You can feel that there's something more. I can.

LACY: I think it's like the feeling we all had when we were singing together.

SARAH: Beautiful.

SAM: Maybe the whole reason we haven't moved on is because we haven't taken the risk.

Lacy and Sam look at each other. Lacy reaches out to hold Sam's hand. They begin the countdown.

ALL: Ten, nine, eight, seven, six . . .

As the countdown continues, everyone joins hands, standing still, looking straight ahead.

ALL: Five, four, three, two, one . . .

The most gorgeous colors begin to rise. Slowly sunlight fills the stage and swells with such beautiful ferocity, we are no longer able to see anything but color.

SCENE 10: THE AMEN

Raven is alone in the day-bright cemetery. The sky behind him is a cloudless blue. A drumroll begins, softly at first and then building. We're not sure where the sound is coming from. Perhaps it is merely the sonic ripple-effect of a truck passing by on a nearby street or perhaps it is the deep thrumming of the invisible cosmic gears that turn the Earth.

Perched on Poe's monument, the bird looks directly at us, black eyes glittering. He opens his beak as if to finally give us the truth, to tell us what it all means, to tell us what that vastness of infinity holds for our characters and holds for us, and then a look—a mixture of humor, pity, and love—flashes from his eyes, and he closes his beak. That thing gathering inside our chests—hope—snags against the prickle of comprehension. We know now that he won't reveal a thing.

As the drumming continues, Raven looks at us for a long moment without blinking. Then he opens his wings fully—more magnificent than we could have ever imagined—and lifts. As our eyes follow his shifting black shape, the light filters through the wings, streaming and changing in intensity and color until we're not sure when we're seeing shadows and when we're seeing light and when we're seeing sky. It's dizzying. Exhilarating.

Gradually we discover that we're looking down now and that we have left the cemetery. We recognize a new scene: an ordinary street in Baltimore . . . a café with tables outside. It is summer. For a moment, we take in the vibrancy of the colors and sounds: the patrons at the tables, the people passing by, the cars, the marquee of the nearby theater, the shops and restaurants, the strollers, the child stopping to pet the dog on a leash. And then we focus on a young woman sitting at one of the small round café tables: Olivia. She is wearing a sleeveless dress, and the skin of her face and arms in the sunlight is smooth and alive.

In front of her is a glass of water and a piece of cinnamon crumb cake on a blue and yellow plate. It is a middle piece. Perfectly baked. Olivia closes her eyes and breathes in the smell. Then, she opens her eyes. With her fingers, she lifts the cake from the plate and takes a bite.

LIGHTS DO NOT FADE.

ACKNOWLEDGMENTS

I am eternally indebted to Alix Reid *[yes, dear Reader, that is the correct spelling of her name]* for saying yes to this odd project and for her willingness to toil on it during the unwieldy early-draft stage. When it was a play of mere sticks and bones, Alix urged me to flesh out the characters, an especially challenging task given the fact that most of them were dead and buried centuries ago.

I also owe my gratitude to Julie Zielke for embracing that antiquated experience known as an actual phone call. Julie has an unusual knack for listening to the dilemmas of characters she has never had the chance to meet and for imparting deep insights about them. I don't know how she does it, but she always has my ear.

For comments on early scenes or drafts, my appreciation extends to Ivan Amato, Andrea Caspari, Bob Hersh, Danny Scheie, Phil Schewe, John Feffer, Jeremy Berlin, Isadora Kaplan, my beloved Hive, the participants and staff of the 2016 National Playwrights' Symposium at Cape May, including playwright Steven Dietz, Shawn Fisher and Roy Steinberg, and my offspring, Max and Simon Amato (the latter of whom must be given an extra dollop of thanks for the termites).

You may all count on me for a favor in return for as long as I live—and, who knows, maybe even after that.